Frank Herbert, one of the all-time giants of science fiction, has been writing for more than twenty years. His work has been translated into many languages and almost all his novels remain continuously in print. His epic science fiction novel *Dune* has won both the Hugo and Nebula awards, and as well as being a world-wide bestseller, it is also considered a classic of the genre. In his work, Frank Herbert has drawn on his studies of Oriental philosophy and undersea geology, as well as his own experiences as a professional photographer, television cameraman, radio news commentator, journalist and lay analyst. An authority on ecology, he has been active as a lecturer and campaigner for the preservation of the world's resources.

D1388797

Also by Frank Herbert

Frank Herbert

The Book
of Frank Herbert

Panther

Granada Publishing Limited
First published in Great Britain in 1977
by Panther Books Ltd
Frogmore, St Albans, Herts AL2 2NF

A Panther UK Original
First published by Daw Books, Inc USA 1973
Copyright © Frank Herbert 1973
Individual stories copyright © 1954, 1955, 1970,
by the Condé Nast Publications, Inc;
1952, by *Startling Stories;*
1954, 1955, by Ultimate Publishing Co;
1956 by *Fantastic Universe*
Made and printed in Great Britain by
Hazell Watson & Viney Ltd
Aylesbury, Bucks
Set in Intertype Times

CONTENTS

SEED STOCK

When the sun had sunk almost to the edge of the purple ocean, hanging there like a giant orange ball – much larger than the sun of Mother Earth which he remembered with such nostalgia – Kroudar brought his fishermen back to the harbor.

A short man, Kroudar gave the impression of heaviness, but under his shipcloth motley he was as scrawny as any of the others, all bone and stringy muscle. It was the sickness of this planet, the doctors told him. They called it 'body burdens,' a subtle thing of differences in chemistry, gravity, diurnal periods and even the lack of a tidal moon.

Kroudar's yellow hair, his one good feature, was uncut and contained in a protective square of red cloth. Beneath this was a wide, low forehead, deeply sunken large eyes of a washed-out blue, a crooked nose that was splayed and pushed in, thick lips over large and unevenly spaced yellow teeth, and a melon chin receding into a short, ridged neck.

Dividing his attention between sails and shore, Kroudar steered with one bare foot on the tiller.

They had been all day out in the up-coast current netting the shrimp-like *trodi* which formed the colony's main source of edible protein. There were nine boats and the men in all of them were limp with fatigue, silent, eyes closed or open and staring at nothing.

The evening breeze rippled its dark lines across the harbor, moved the sweat-matted yellow hair on Kroudar's neck. It bellied the shipcloth sails and gave the heavily loaded boats that last necessary surge to carry them up into the strand.

Men moved then. Sails dropped with a slatting and rasping. Each thing was done with sparse motion in the weighted slowness of their fatigue.

Trodi had been thick in the current out there, and Krou-

7

dar pushed his people to their limit. It had not taken much
push. They all understood the need. The swarmings and
runnings of useful creatures on this planet had not been
clocked with any reliable precision. Things here exhibited
strange gaps and breaks in seeming regularity. The *trodi*
might vanish at any moment into some unknown place –
as they had been known to do before.

The colony had experienced hunger and children crying
for food that must be rationed. Men seldom spoke of this
any more, but they moved with the certain knowledge of it.

More than three years now, Kroudar thought, as he
shouldered a dripping bag of *trodi* and pushed his weary
feet through the sand, climbing the beach toward the storage huts and racks where the sea creatures were dried for
processing. It had been more than three years since their
ship had come down from space.

The colony ship had been constructed as a multiple tool,
filled with select human stock, their domestic animals and
basic necessities, and it had been sent to plant humans in
this far place. It had been designed to land once, then be
broken down into useful things.

Somehow, the basic necessities had fallen short, and the
colony had been forced to improvise its own tools. They
had not really settled here yet, Kroudar realized. More than
three years – and three years here were five years of Mother
Earth – and they still lived on the edge of extinction. They
were trapped here. Yes, that was true. The ship could never
be reconstructed. And even if that miracle were accom-
plished, the fuel did not exist.

The colony was *here*.

And every member knew the predatory truth of their
predicament: survival had not been assured. It was known
in subtle things to Kroudar's unlettered mind, especially in
a fact he observed without being able to explain.

Not one of their number had yet accepted a name for
this planet. It was 'here' or 'this place.'

Or even more bitter terms.

* * *

Kroudar dumped his sack of *trodi* onto a storage hut porch, mopped his forehead. The joints of his arms and legs ached. His back ached. He could feel the sickness of *this place* in his bowels. Again, he wiped perspiration from his forehead, removed the red cloth he wore to protect his head from that brutal sun.

Yellow hair fell down as he loosed the cloth, and he swung the hair back over his shoulders.

It would be dark very soon.

The red cloth was dirty, he saw. It would require another gentle washing. Kroudar thought it odd, this cloth: grown and woven on Mother Earth, it would end its days on *this place*.

Even as he and the others.

He stared at the cloth for a moment before placing it carefully in a pocket.

All around him, his fishermen were going through the familiar ritual. Brown sacks woven of coarse native roots were dumped dripping onto the storage hut porches. Some of his men leaned then against the porch uprights, some sprawled in the sand.

Kroudar lifted his gaze. Fires behind the bluff above them sent smoke spirals into the darkening sky. Kroudar was suddenly hungry. He thought of Technician Honida up there at the cookfire, their twin sons – two years old next week – nearby at the door of the shipmetal longhouse.

It stirred him to think of Honida. She had chosen *him*. With men from the Scientist class and the Technicians available to her, Honida had reached down into the Labor pool to tap the one they all called 'Old Ugly.' He wasn't old, Kroudar reminded himself. But he knew the source of the name. *This place* had worked its changes on him with more visible evidence than upon any of the others.

Kroudar held no illusions about why he had been brought on this human migration. It was his muscles and his minimal education. The reason was embodied in that label written down in the ship manifest – laborer. The planners back on Mother Earth had realized there were tasks which required human muscles not inhibited by too much thinking. The *kroudars* landed *here* were not numerous, but they knew each other and they knew themselves for what they were.

There'd even been talk among the higher echelons of not allowing Honida to choose him as mate. Kroudar knew this. He did not resent it particularly. It didn't even bother him that the vote among the biologists – they'd discussed his ugliness at great length, so it was reported – favored Honida's choice on philosophical rather than physical grounds.

Kroudar knew he was ugly.

He knew also that his present hunger was a good sign. A strong desire to see his family grew in him, beginning to ignite his muscles for the climb from the beach. Particularly, he wanted to see his twins, the one yellow-haired like himself, and the other dark as Honida. The other women favored with children looked down upon his twins as stunted and sickly, Kroudar knew. The women fussed over diets and went running to the medics almost every day. But as long as Honida did not worry, Kroudar remained calm. Honida, after all, was a technician, a worker in the hydroponics gardens.

Kroudar moved his bare feet softly in the sand. Once more, he looked up at the bluff. Along the edge grew scattered native trees. Their thick trunks hugged the ground, gnarled and twisted, supports for bulbous, yellow-green leaves that exuded poisonous milky sap in the heat of the day. A few of the surviving Earth-falcons perched in the trees, silent, watchful.

The birds gave Kroudar an odd confidence in his own decisions. For what do the falcons watch, he wondered. It was a question the most exalted of the colony's thinkers had not been able to answer. Search 'copters had been sent out following the falcons. The birds flew offshore in the night, rested occasionally on barren islands, and returned at dawn. The colony command had been unwilling to risk its precious boats in the search, and the mystery of the falcons remained unsolved.

It was doubly a mystery because the other birds had perished or flown off to some unfound place. The doves, the quail – the gamebirds and songbirds – all had vanished. And the domestic chickens had all died, their eggs infertile. Kroudar knew this as a comment by *this place*, a warning for the life that came from Mother Earth.

A few scrawny cattle survived, and several calves had been born *here*. But they moved with a listless gait and there was distressed lowing in the pastures. Looking into their eyes was like looking into open wounds. A few pigs still lived, as listless and sickly as the cattle, and all the wild creatures had strayed off or died.

Except the falcons.

How odd it was, because the people who planned and conceived profound thoughts had held such hopes for *this place*. The survey reports had been exciting. This was a planet without native land animals. It was a planet whose native plants appeared not too different from those of Mother Earth – in some respects. And the sea creatures were primitive by sophisticated evolutionary standards.

Without being able to put it into those beautifully polished phrases which others admired, Kroudar knew where the mistake had been made. Sometimes, you had to search out a problem with your flesh and not with your mind.

He stared around now at the motley rags of his men. They were *his* men. He was the master fisherman, the one who had found the *trodi* and conceived these squat, ugly boats built within the limitations of native woods. The colony was alive now because of his skills with boat and net.

There would be more gaps in the *trodi* runs, though. Kroudar felt this as an awareness on the edges of his fatigue. There would be unpopular and dangerous things to do then, all necessary because *thinking* had failed. The salmon they had introduced, according to plan, had gone off into the ocean vastness. The flatfish in the colony's holding ponds suffered mysterious attrition. Insects flew away and were never seen again.

There's food here, the biologists argued. Why do they die?

The colony's maize was a sometime thing with strange ears. Wheat came up in scabrous patches. There were no familiar patterns of growth or migration. The colony lived on the thin edge of existence, maintained by protein bulk from the processed *trodi* and vitamins from vegetables grown hydroponically with arduous filtering and adjustment of their water. Breakdown of a single system in the chain could bring disaster.

The giant orange sun showed only a small arc above the sea horizon now, and Kroudar's men were stirring themselves, lifting their tired bodies off the sand, pushing away from the places where they had leaned.

'All right now,' Kroudar ordered. 'Let's get this food inside on the racks.'

'Why?' someone asked from the dusk: 'You think the falcons will eat it?'

They all knew the falcons would not eat the *trodi*. Kroudar recognized the objection: it was tiredness of the mind speaking. The shrimp creatures fed only humans – after careful processing to remove dangerous irritants. A falcon might take up a frond-legged *trodi*, but would drop it at the first taste.

What did they eat, those waiting birds?

Falcons knew a thing about *this place* that humans did not know. The birds knew it in their flesh in the way Kroudar sought the knowledge.

Darkness fell, and with a furious clatter, the falcons flew off toward the sea. One of Kroudar's men kindled a torch and, having rested, anxious now to climb the bluff and join their families, the fishermen pitched into the work that must be done. Boats were hauled up on rollers. *Trodi* were spread out in thin layers along racks within the storage huts. Nets were draped on racks to dry.

As he worked, Kroudar wondered about the scientists up there in the shining laboratories. He had the working man's awe of knowledge, a servility in the face of titles and things clearly superior, but he had also the simple man's sure awareness of when superior things failed.

Kroudar was not privy to the high-level conferences in the colony command, but he knew the physical substance of the ideas discussed there. His awareness of failure and hovering disaster had no sophisticated words or erudition to hold itself dancingly before men's minds, but his knowledge carried its own elegance. He drew on ancient knowledge adjusted subtly to the differences of *this place*. Kroudar had found the *trodi*. Kroudar had organized the methods of capturing them and preserving them. He had no refined labels to explain it, but Kroudar knew himself for what he could do and what he was.

He was the first sea peasant *here*.

Without wasting energy on talk, Kroudar's band finished the work, turned away from the storage huts and plodded up the cliff trail, their course marked by, here and there, men with flaming torches. There were fuzzy orange lights, heavy shadows, inching their way upward in a black world, and they gave heart to Kroudar.

Lingering to the last, he checked the doors of the huts, then followed, hurrying to catch up. The man directly ahead of him on the path carried a torch, native wood soaked in *trodi* oil. It flickered and smoked and gave off poisonous fumes. The light revealed a troglodyte figure, a human clad in patched shipcloth, body too thin, muscles moving on the edge of collapse.

Kroudar sighed.

It was not like this on Mother Earth, he knew. There, the women waited on the strand for their men to return from the sea. Children played among the pebbles. Eager hands helped with the work onshore, spreading the nets, carrying the catch, pulling the boats.

Not *here*.

And the perils *here* were not the perils of Home. Kroudar's boats never strayed out of sight of these cliffs. One boat always carried a technician with a radio for contact with shore. Before its final descent, the colony ship had seeded space with orbiting devices – watchers, guardians against surprises from the weather. The laboriously built fishing fleet always had ample warning of storms. No monster sea creatures had ever been seen in that ocean.

This place lacked the cruel savagery and variety of seas Kroudar had known, but it was nonetheless deadly. He *knew* this.

The women should wait for us on the shore, he thought.

But colony command said the women – and even some of the children – were needed for too many other tasks. Individual plants from home required personal attention. Single wheat stalks were nurtured with tender care. Each orchard tree existed with its own handmaiden, its guardian dryad.

Atop the cliff, the fishermen came in sight of the long-houses, shipmetal *quonsets* named for some far distant place and time in human affairs. Scattered electric lights ringed the town. Many of the unpaved streets wandered off unlit. There were mechanical sounds here and murmurous voices.

The men scattered to their own affairs now, no longer a band. Kroudar plodded down his street toward the open cook fires in the central plaza. The open fires were a necessity to conserve the more sophisticated energies of the colony. Some looked upon those flames as admission of defeat. Kroudar saw them as victory. It was *native* wood being burned.

Off in the hills beyond the town, he knew, stood the ruins of the wind machines they had built. The storm which had wreaked that destruction had achieved no surprise in its coming, but had left enormous surprise at its power.

For Kroudar, the *thinkers* had begun to diminish in

stature then. When native chemistry and water life had wrecked the turbines in the river which emptied into the harbor, those men of knowledge had shrunk even more. Then it was that Kroudar had begun his own search for native foods.

Now, Kroudar heard, native plant life threatened the cooling systems for their atomic generators, defying radiation in a way no life should. Some among the technicians already were fashioning steam engines of materials not intended for such use. Soon, they would have native metals, though – materials to resist the wild etchings and rusts of *this place*.

They might succeed – provided the dragging sickness did not sap them further.

If they survived.

Honida awaited him at the door to their quarters, smiling, graceful. Her dark hair was plaited and wound in rings around her forehead. The brown eyes were alive with welcome. Firelight from the plaza cast a familiar glow across her olive skin. The high cheekbones of her Amerind ancestry, the full lips and proudly hooked nose – all filled him with remembered excitement.

Kroudar wondered if the *planners* had known this thing about her which gave him such warmth – her strength and fecundity. She had chosen *him*, and now she carried more of their children – twins again.

'Ahhh, my fisherman is home,' she said, embracing him in the doorway for anybody to see.

They went inside then, closed the door, and she held him with more ardor, stared up into his face which, reflected in her eyes, lost some of its ugliness.

'Honida,' he said, unable to find other words.

Presently, he asked about the boys.

'They're asleep,' she said, leading him to the crude trestle table he had built for their kitchen.

He nodded. Later, he would go in and stare at his sons.

It did not bother him that they slept so much. He could feel the reasons for this somewhere within himself.

Honida had hot *trodi* soup waiting for him on the table. It was spiced with hydroponic tomatoes and peas and contained other things which he knew she gathered from the land without telling the scientists.

Whatever she put in front of him, Kroudar ate. There was bread tonight with an odd musty flavor which he found pleasant. In the light of the single lamp they were permitted for this room, he stared at a piece of the bread. It was almost purple – like the sea. He chewed it, swallowed.

Honida, watchfully eating across from him, finished her bread and soup, asked: 'Do you like the bread?'

'I like it.'

'I made it myself in the coals,' she said.

He nodded, took another slice.

Honida refilled his soup bowl.

They were privileged, Kroudar realized, to have this privacy for their meals. Many of the others had opted for communal cooking and eating – even among the technicians and higher echelons who possessed more freedom of choice. Honida had seen something about *this place*, though, which required secrecy and going private ways.

Kroudar, hunger satisfied, stared across the table at her. He adored her with a devotion that went far deeper than the excitement of her flesh. He could not say the thing she was, but he knew it. If they were to have a future here, that future was in Honida and the things he might learn, form and construct of himself with his own flesh.

Under the pressure of his eyes, Honida arose, came around the table and began massaging the muscles of his back – the very muscles he used to haul the nets.

'You're tired,' she said. 'Was it difficult out there today?'

'Hard work,' Kroudar said.

He admired the way she spoke. She had many words at her disposal. He had heard her use some of them during colony meetings and during the time of their application for mating choice. She had words for things he did not know, and she knew also when to speak with her body rather than with her mouth. She knew about the muscles of his back.

Kroudar felt such a love for her then that he wondered if it went up through her fingers into her body.

'We filled the boats,' he said.

'I was told today that we'll soon need more storage huts,' she said. 'They're worried about sparing the labor for the building.'

'Ten more huts,' he said.

She would pass that word along, he knew. Somehow it would be done. The other technicians listened to Honida. Many among the scientists scoffed at her; it could be heard beneath the blandness of their voices. Perhaps it was because she had chosen Kroudar for mate. But technicians listened. The huts would be built.

And they would be filled before the *trodi* run stopped.

Kroudar realized then that he knew when the run would stop, not as a date, but almost as a physical thing which he could reach out and touch. He longed for the words to explain this to Honida.

She gave his back a final kneading, sat down beside him and leaned her dark head against his chest. 'If you're not too tired,' she said, 'I have something to show you.'

With a feeling of surprise, Kroudar became aware of unspoken excitement in Honida. Was it something about the hydroponic gardens where she worked? His thoughts went immediately to that place upon which the scientists pinned their hopes, the place where they chose the tall plants, the beautiful, engorged with richness from Mother Earth. Had they achieved something important at last? Was there, after all, a clear way to make *this place* arable?

Kroudar was a primitive then wanting his gods redeemed. He found himself full of peasant hopes for the land. Even a sea peasant knew the value of land.

He and Honida had responsibilities, though. He nodded questioningly toward the twins' bedroom.

'I arranged . . .' She gestured toward their neighbor's cubicle. 'They will listen.'

She had planned this, then. Kroudar stood up, held out his hand for her. 'Show me.'

They went out into the night. Their town was quieter now; he could hear the distant roistering of the river. For a moment, he thought he heard a cricket, but reason told him it could only be one of the huts cooling in the night. He longed wordlessly for a moon.

Honida had brought one of the rechargeable electric torches, the kind issued to technicians against emergency calls in the night. Seeing that torch, Kroudar sensed a deeper importance in this mysterious thing she wanted to show him. Honida had the peasant's hoarding instinct. She would not waste such a torch.

Instead of leading him toward the green lights and glass roofs of the hydroponic gardens, though, she guided their steps in the opposite direction toward the deep gorge where the river plunged into the harbor.

There were no guards along the footpath, only an occasional stone marker and grotesqueries of native growth. Swiftly, without speaking, she led him to the gorge and the narrow path which he knew went only down to a ledge which jutted into the damp air of the river's spray.

Kroudar found himself trembling with excitement as he followed Honida's shadowy figure, the firefly darting of her light. It was cold on the ledge and the alien outline of native trees revealed by the torch filled Kroudar with disquiet.

What had Honida discovered – or created?

Condensation dripped from the plants here. The river noise was loud. It was marsh air he breathed, dank and filled with bizarre odors.

Honida stopped, and Kroudar held his breath. He listened. There was only the river.

For a moment, he didn't realize that Honida was directing the orange light of the torch at her discovery. It looked like one of the native plants – a thing with a thick stem crouched low to the land, gnarled and twisted, bulbous yellow-green protrusions set with odd spacing along its length.

Slowly, realization came over him. He recognized a darker tone in the green, the way the leaf structures were joined to the stalk, a bunching of brown-yellow silk drooping from the bulbous protrusions.

'Maize,' he whispered.

In a low voice, pitching her explanation to Kroudar's vocabulary, Honida explained what she had done. He saw it in her words, understood why she had done this thing stealthily, here away from the scientists. He took the light from her, crouched, stared with rapt attention. This meant the death of those things the scientists held beautiful. It ended their plan for *this place*.

Kroudar could see his own descendants in this plant. They might develop bulbous heads, hairless, wide thick-lipped mouths. Their skins might become purple. They would be short statured; he knew that.

Honida had assured this – right here on the river-drenched ledge. Instead of selecting seed from the tallest, the straightest stalks, the ones with the longest and most perfect ears – the ones most like those from Mother Earth – she had tested her maize almost to destruction. She had chosen sickly, scrawny plants, ones barely able to produce seed. She had taken only those plants which *this place* influenced most deeply. From these, she had selected finally a strain which lived *here* as native plants lived.

This was *native* maize.

She broke off an ear, peeled back the husk.

There were gaps in the seed rows and, when she squeezed a kernel, the juice ran purple. He recognized the smell of the bread.

Here was the thing the scientists would not admit. They were trying to make *this place* into another Earth. But it was not and it could never be. The falcons had been the first among their creatures to discover this, he suspected.

The statement Honida made here was that she and Kroudar would be short-lived. Their children would be sickly by Mother Earth's standards. Their descendants would change in ways that defied the hopes of those who had planned this migration. The scientists would hate this and try to stop it.

This gnarled stalk of maize said the scientists would fail.

For a long while, Kroudar crouched there, staring into the future until the torch began to dim, losing its charge. He aroused himself then, led the way back out of the gorge.

At the top, with the lights of their dying civilization visible across the plain, he stopped, said: 'The *trodi* run will stop . . . soon. I will take one boat and . . . friends. We will go out where the falcons go.'

It was one of the longest speeches he had ever made.

She took the light from his hand, extinguished it, pressed herself against him.

'What do you think the falcons have found?'

'The seed,' he said.

He shook his head. He could not explain it, but the thing was there in his awareness. Everything here exuded poisonous vapors, or juices in which only its own seed could live. Why should the *trodi* or any other sea creature be different? And, with the falcons as evidence, the seed must be slightly less poisonous to the intruders from Mother Earth.

'The boats are slow,' she said.

He agreed silently. A storm could trap them too far out for a run to safety. It would be dangerous. But he heard also in her voice that she was not trying to stop him or dissuade him.

'I will take good men,' he said.

'How long will you be gone?' Honida asked.

He thought about this for a moment. The rhythms of *this place* were beginning to make themselves known to him. His awareness shaped the journey, the days out, the night search over the water where the falcons were known to sweep in their low guiding runs – then the return.

'Eight days,' he said.

'You'll need fine mesh nets,' she said. 'I'll see to having them made. Perhaps a few technicians, too. I know some who will go with you.'

'Eight days,' he said, telling her to choose strong men.

'Yes,' she said. 'Eight days. I'll be waiting on the shore when you return.'

He took her hand then and led the way back across the plain. As they walked, he said: 'We must name *this place*.'

'When you come back,' she said.

THE NOTHING

If it hadn't been for the fight with my father I'd never have gone down to the Tavern and then I wouldn't have met the *Nothing*. This *Nothing* was really just an ordinary looking guy. He wasn't worth special attention unless, like me, you were pretending you were Marla Graim, the feelies star, and him Sidney Harch meeting you in the bar to give you a spy capsule.

It was all my father's fault. Imagine him getting angry because I wouldn't take a job burning brush. What kind of work is that for an eighteen-year-old girl anyway? I know my folks were hard pressed for money but that was no excuse for the way he lit into me.

We had the fight over lunch but it was after six o'clock before I got the chance to sneak out of the house. I went down to the Tavern because I knew the old man would be madder than a tele in a lead barrel when he found out. There was no way I could keep it from him, of course. He pried me every time I came home.

The Tavern is a crossroads place where the talent gets together to compare notes, and talk about jobs. I'd only been in there once before, and that time with my father. He warned me not to go there alone because a lot of the jags used the place. You could smell the stuff all over the main room. There was pink smoke from a hyro bowl drifting up around the rafters. Someone had a Venusian Oin filter going. There was a lot of talent there for so early in the evening.

I found an empty corner of the bar and ordered a blue fire because I'd seen Marla Graim ask for one in the feelies. The bartender stared at me sharply and I suspected he was a tele, but he didn't pry. After awhile he floated my drink up to me and 'ported away my money. I sipped the drink the way I'd seen Marla Graim do, but it was too sweet. I tried not to let my face show anything.

The bar mirror gave me a good broad view of the room and I kept looking into it as though I was expecting somebody. Then this big blond young man came through the front door. I saw him in the mirror and immediately knew he was going to take the seat beside me. I'm not exactly a prescient, but sometimes those things are obvious.

He came across the room, moving with a gladiator ease between the packed tables. That's when I pretended I was Marla Graim waiting at a Port Said bar to pick up a spy capsule from Sidney Harch like in the feelie I'd seen Sunday. This fellow did look a little like Harch – curly hair, dark blue eyes, face all sharp angles as if it had been chiseled by a sculptor who'd left the job uncompleted.

He took the stool beside me as I'd known he would, and ordered a blue fire, easy on the sugar. Naturally, I figured this was a get-acquainted gambit and wondered what to say to him. Suddenly, it struck me as an exciting idea to just ride along with the Marla Graim plot until it came time to leave.

He couldn't do anything to stop me even if he was a 'porter. You see, I'm a pyro and that's a good enough defense for anyone. I glanced down at my circa-twenty skirt and shifted until the slit exposed my garter the way I'd seen Marla Graim do it. This blond lad didn't give it a tumble. He finished his drink, and ordered another.

I whiffed him for one of the cokes, but he was dry. No jag. The other stuff in the room was getting through to me, though, and I was feeling dizzy. I knew I'd have to leave soon and I'd never get another chance to be a Marla Graim type; so I said, 'What's yours?'

Oh, he knew I was talking to him all right, but he didn't even look up. It made me mad. A girl has some pride and there I'd unbent enough to start the conversation! There was an ashtray piled with scraps of paper in front of him. I concentrated on it and the paper suddenly flamed. I'm a good pyro when I want to be. Some men have been kind enough to say I could start a fire without the talent. But with a prying father like mine how could I ever know?

The fire got this fellow's attention. He knew I'd started it. He just glanced at me once and turned away. 'Leave me alone,' he said. 'I'm a *Nothing*.'

I don't know what it was. Maybe I have a little of the tele like that doctor said once, but I knew he was telling the truth. It wasn't one of those gags like you see in the feelies. You know – where there are two comedians and one says, 'What's yours?' And the other one answers, 'Nothing.'

Only all the time he's levitating the other guy's chair and juggling half a dozen things behind his back, no hands. You know the gag. It's been run into the ground. Well, when he said that, it kind of set me back. I'd never seen a real-life *Nothing* before. Oh, I knew there were some. In the government preserves and such, but I'd never been like this – right next to one.

'Sorry,' I said. 'I'm a pyro.'

He glanced at the ashes in the tray and said, 'Yeah, I know.'

'There's not much work for pyros any more,' I said. 'It's the only talent I have.' I turned and looked at him. Handsome in spite of being a *Nothing*. 'What did you do?' I asked.

'I ran away,' he said. 'I'm a fugitive from the Sonoma Preserve.'

That made my blood tingle. Not only a *Nothing*, but a fugitive, too. Just like in the feelies. I said, 'Do you want to hide out at my place?'

That brought him around. He looked me over and he actually blushed. Actually! I'd never seen a man blush before. That fellow certainly was loaded with firsts for me.

'People might get the wrong idea when I'm caught,' he said. 'I'm sure to be caught eventually. I always am.'

I was really getting a feeling for that woman-of-the-world part. 'Why not enjoy your freedom then?' I asked.

I let him see a little more through the circa-twenty slit. He actually turned away! Imagine!

That's when the police came. They didn't make any fuss. I'd noticed these two men standing just inside the door watching us. Only I'd thought they were watching me. They came across the room and one of them bent over this fellow.

'All right, Claude,' he said. 'Come quietly.'

The other took my arm and said, 'You'll have to come, too, sister.'

I jerked away from him. 'I'm not your sister,' I said.

'Oh, leave her alone, fellows,' said this Claude. 'I didn't tell her anything. She was just trying to pick me up.'

'Sorry,' said the cop. 'She comes, too.'

That's when I began to get scared. 'Look,' I said. 'I don't know what this is all about.'

The man showed me the snout of a hypo gun in his pocket. 'Stop the commotion and come quietly, sister, or I'll have to use this,' he said.

So who wants to go to sleep? I went quietly, praying we'd run into my father or someone I knew so I could explain things. But no such luck.

The police had a plain old jet buggy outside with people clustered around looking at it. A 'porter in the crowd was having fun jiggling the rear end up and down off the ground. He was standing back with his hands in his pockets, grinning.

The cop who'd done all the talking just looked toward this 'porter and the fellow lost his grin and hurried away. I knew then the cop was a tele, although he hadn't touched my mind. They're awfully sensitive about their code of ethics, some of those teles.

It was fun riding in that old jet buggy. I'd never been in one before. One of the cops got in back with Claude and me. The other one drove. It was the strangest feeling, flying up over the bay on the tractors. Usually, whenever I wanted to go someplace, I'd just ask, polite like, was there a 'porter around and then I'd think of where I wanted to go and the 'porter would set me down there quick as a wink.

Of course, I wound up in some old gent's apartment now and then. Some 'porters do that sort of thing for a fee. But a pyro doesn't have to worry about would-be Casanovas. No old gent is going to fool around when his clothes are on fire.

Well, the jet buggy finally set down on an old hospital grounds way back up in the sticks and the cops took us to the main building and into a little office. Walking, mind you. It was shady in the office – not enough lights – and it took a minute for my eyes to adjust after the bright lights in the hall. When they did adjust and I saw the old codger behind the desk I did a real double take. It was Mensor Williams. Yeah. The *Big All*. Anything anybody else can do he can do better.

Somebody worked a switch somewhere and the lights brightened. 'Good evening, Miss Carlysle,' he said and his little goatee bobbled.

Before I could make a crack about ethics against reading minds, he said, 'I'm not intruding into your mental processes. I've merely scanned forward to a point where I learn your name.'

A prescient, too!

'There really wasn't any need to bring her,' he told the cops. 'But it was inevitable that you would.' Then he did the funniest thing. He turned to Claude and nodded his head toward me. 'How do you like her, Claude?' he asked. Just like I was something offered for sale or something!

Claude said, 'Is she the one, Dad?'

Dad! That one smacked me. The *Big All* has a kid and the kid's a *Nothing!*

'She's the one,' said Williams.

Claude kind of squared his shoulders and said, 'Well, I'm going to throw a stick into the works. I won't do it!'

'Yes, you will,' said Williams.

This was all way over my head and I'd had about enough

anyway. I said, 'Now wait a minute, gentlemen, or I'll set the place on fire! I mean literally!'

'She can do it, too,' said Claude, grinning at his father.

'But she won't,' said Williams.

'Oh, won't I?' I said. 'Well, you just try and stop me!'

'No need to do that,' said Williams. 'I've seen what's going to happen.'

Just like that! These prescients give me the creeps. Sometimes I wonder if they don't give themselves the creeps. Living for them must be like repeating a part you already know. Not for me. I said. 'What would happen if I did something different from what you'd seen?'

Williams leaned forward with an interested look in his eyes. 'It's never happened,' he said. 'If it did happen once, that'd be a real precedent.'

I can't be sure, but looking at him there, I got the idea he'd really be interested to see something happen different from his forecast. I thought of starting a little fire, maybe in the papers on his desk. But somehow the idea didn't appeal to me. It wasn't that any presence was in my mind telling me not to. I don't know exactly what it was. I just didn't *want* to do it. I said, 'What's the meaning of all this double talk?'

The old man leaned back and I swear he seemed kind of disappointed. He said, 'It's just that you and Claude are going to be married.'

I opened my mouth to speak and nothing came out. Finally, I managed to stammer, 'You mean you've looked into the future and seen us *married?* How many kids we're going to have and everything like that?'

'Well, not everything,' he said. 'All things in the future aren't clear to us. Only certain main-line developments. And we can't see too far into the future for most things. The past is easier. That's been fixed immovably.'

'And what if we don't want to?' asked Claude.

'Yeah,' I said. 'What about that?' But I have to admit the idea wasn't totally repulsive. As I've said, Claude looked like Sidney Harch, only younger. He had something – you can call it animal magnetism if you wish.

The old man just smiled. 'Miss Carlysle,' he said, 'do you honestly object to—'

'As long as I'm going to be in the family you can call me Jean,' I said.

I was beginning to feel fatalistic about the whole thing. My great aunt Harriet was a prescient and I'd had experience with them. Now I was remembering the time she told me my kitty was going to die and I hid it in the old cistern and that night it rained and filled the cistern. Naturally the kitty drowned. I never forgave her for not telling me how the kitty was going to die.

Old Williams looked at me and said, 'At least *you're* being reasonable.'

'I'm not,' said Claude.

So I told them about my great aunt Harriet.

'It's the nature of things,' said Williams. 'Why can't you be as reasonable as she's being, son?'

Claude just sat there with the original stone face.

'Am I so repulsive?' I asked.

He looked at me then. Really looked. I tell you I got warm under it. I know I'm not repulsive. Finally, I guess I blushed.

'You're not repulsive,' he said. 'I just object to having my whole life ordered out for me like a chess set up.'

Stalemate. We sat there for a minute or so, completely silent. Presently Williams turned to me and said, 'Well, Miss Carlysle, I presume you're curious about what's going on here.'

'I'm not a moron,' I said. 'This is one of the *Nothing* Preserves.'

'Correct,' he said. 'Only it's more than that. Your education includes the knowledge of how our talents developed from radiation mutants. Does it also include the knowledge of what happens to extremes from the norm?'

Every schoolkid knows that, of course. So I told him. Sure I knew that the direction of development was toward the average. That genius parents tend to have children less smart than they are. This is just general information.

Then the old man threw me the twister. 'The talents are disappearing, my dear,' he said.

I just sat there and thought about that for awhile. Certainly I knew it'd been harder lately to get a 'porter, even one of the old gent kind.

'Each generation has more children without talents or with talents greatly dulled,' said Williams. 'We will never reach a point where there are absolutely none, but what few remain will be needed for special jobs in the public interest.'

'You mean if I have kids they're liable to be *Nothings?*' I asked.

'Look at your own family,' he said. 'Your great aunt was a prescient. Have there been any others in your family?'

'Well, no, but—'

'The prescient talent is an extreme,' he said. 'There are fewer than a thousand left. There are nine of us in my category. I believe you refer to us as the *Big All.*'

'But we've got to do something!' I said. 'The world'll just go to pot!'

'We *are* doing something,' he said. 'Right here and on eight other preserves scattered around the world. We're reviving the mechanical and tool skills which supported the pretalent civilization and we're storing the instruments which will make a rebirth of that civilization possible.'

He raised a warning hand. 'But we must move in secrecy. The world's not yet ready for this information. It would cause a most terrible panic if this were to become known.'

'Well, you're prescient. What does happen?' I asked him.

'Unfortunately, none of us are able to determine that,' he said. 'Either it's an unfixed line or there's some interference which we can't surmount.' He shook his head and the goatee wiggled. 'There's a cloudy area in the near future beyond which we can't see. None of us.'

That scared me. A prescient may give you the creeps,

but it's nice to know there's a future into which someone can see. It was as if there suddenly wasn't any future – period. I began to cry a little.

'And our children will be *Nothings*,' I said.

'Well, not exactly,' said Williams. 'Some of them, maybe, but we've taken the trouble of comparing your gene lines – yours and Claude's. You've a good chance of having offspring who will be prescient or telepathic or both. A better than seventy percent chance.' His voice got pleading. 'The world's going to need that chance.'

Claude came over and put a hand on my shoulder. It sent a delicious tingle up my spine. Suddenly, I got a little flash of his thoughts – a picture of us kissing. I'm not really a tele, but like I said, sometimes I get glimmers.

Claude said, 'Okay. I guess there's no sense fighting the inevitable. We'll get married.'

No more argument. We all traipsed into another room and there was a preacher with everything ready for us, even the ring. Another prescient. He'd come more than a hundred miles to perform the ceremony, he said.

Afterward, I let Claude kiss me once. I was having trouble realizing that I was married. Mrs Claude Williams. But that's the way it is with the inevitable, I guess.

The old man took my arm then and said there was one small precaution. I'd be going off the grounds from time to time and there'd always be the chance of some unethical tele picking my brains.

They put me under an anesthetube and when I came out of it I had a silver grid in my skull. It itched some, but they said that it would go away. I'd heard of this thing. They called it a blanket.

Mensor Williams said, 'Now go home and get your things. You won't need to tell your parents any more than that you have a government job. Come back as soon as you're able.'

'Get me a 'porter,' I said.

'The grounds are gridded against teleporters,' he said. 'I'll have to send you in a jet buggy.'

And so he did.

I was home in ten minutes.

I went up the stairs to my house. It was after nine o'clock by then. My father was waiting inside the door.

'A fine time for an eighteen-year-old girl to be coming home!' he shouted and he made a tele stab at my mind to see what I'd been up to. These teles and their ethics! Well, he ran smack dab into the blanket and maybe you think that didn't set him back on his heels. He got all quiet suddenly.

I said, 'I have a government job. I just came back for my things.' Time enough to tell them about the marriage later. They'd have kicked up a fine rumpus if I'd said anything then.

Mama came in and said, 'My little baby with a government job! How much does it pay?'

I said, 'Let's not be vulgar.'

Papa sided with me. 'Of course not, Hazel,' he said. 'Leave the kid alone. A government job! What do you know! Those things pay plenty. Where is it, baby?'

I could see him wondering how much he could tap me for to pay his bills and I began to wonder if I'd have any money at all to keep up the pretense. I said, 'The job's at Sonoma Preserve.'

Papa said, 'What they need with a pyro up there?'

I got a brilliant inspiration. I said, 'To keep the *Nothings* in line. A little burn here, a little burn there. You know.'

That struck my father as funny. When he could stop laughing he said, 'I know you, honey. I've watched your think tank pretty close. You'll take care of yourself and no funny business. Do they have nice safe quarters for you up there?'

'The safest,' I said.

I felt him take another prod at my blanket and withdraw. 'Government work is top secret,' I said.

'Sure. I understand,' he said.

So I went to my room and got my things packed. The

folks made some more fuss about my going away so sudden, but they quieted down when I told them I had to go at once or lose the chance at the job.

Papa finally said, 'Well, if the government isn't safe, then nothing is.'

They kissed me goodbye and I promised to write and to visit home on my first free weekend.

'Don't worry, Papa,' I said.

The jet buggy took me back to the preserve. When I went into the office, Claude, my husband, was sitting across the desk from his father.

The old man had his hands to his forehead and there were beads of perspiration showing where the fingers didn't cover. Presently, he lowered his hands and shook his head.

'Well?' asked Claude.

'Not a thing,' said the old man.

I moved a little bit into the room but they didn't notice me.

'Tell me the truth, Dad,' said Claude. 'How far ahead did you see us?'

Old Mensor Williams lowered his head and sighed. 'All right, son,' he said. 'You deserve the truth. I saw you meet Miss Carlysle at the Tavern and not another thing. We had to trace her by old-fashioned methods and compare your gene lines like I said. The rest is truth. You know I wouldn't lie to you.'

I cleared my throat and they both looked at me.

Claude jumped out of his chair and faced me. 'We can get an annulment,' he said. 'No one has the right to play with other peoples' lives like that.'

He looked so sweet and little-boy-like standing there. I knew suddenly I didn't want an annulment. I said, 'The younger generation has to accept its responsibilities sometime.'

Mensor Williams got an eager look in his eyes. I turned to the old man, said, 'Was that seventy percent figure correct?'

'Absolutely correct, my dear,' he said. 'We've checked

every marriageable female he's met because he carries my family's dominant line. Your combination was the best. Far higher than we'd hoped for.'

'Is there anything else you can tell us about our future?' I asked.

He shook his head. 'It's all cloudy,' he said. 'You're on your own.'

I got that creepy feeling again and looked up at my husband. Little laugh wrinkles creased at the corners of Claude's eyes and he smiled. Then another thought struck me. If we were on our own, that meant we were shaping our own future. It wasn't fixed. And no nosey prescient could come prying in on us, either. A woman kind of likes that idea. Especially on her wedding night.

RAT RACE

In the nine years it took Welby Lewis to become chief of criminal investigation for Sheriff John Czernak, he came to look on police work as something like solving jigsaw puzzles. It was a routine of putting pieces together into a recognizable picture. He was not prepared to have his cynical police-peopled world transformed into a situation out of H. G. Wells or Charles Fort.

When Lewis said 'alien' he meant non-American, not extraterrestrial. Oh, he knew a BEM was a bug-eyed monster; he read some science fiction. But that was just the point – such situations were *fiction*, not to be encountered in police routine. And certainly unexpected at a mortuary. The Johnson-Tule Mortuary, to be exact.

Lewis checked in at his desk in the sheriff's office at five minutes to eight of a Tuesday morning. He was a man of low forehead, thin pinched-in Welsh face, black hair. His eyes were like two pieces of roving green jade glinting beneath bushy brows.

The office, a room of high ceilings and stained plaster walls was in a first floor corner of the County Building at Banbury. Beneath one tall window of the room was a cast-iron radiator. Beside the window hung a calendar picture of a girl wearing only a string of pearls. There were two desks facing each other across an aisle which led from the hall door to the radiator. The desk on the left belonged to Joe Welch, the night man. Lewis occupied the one on the right, a cigarette-scarred vintage piece which had stood in this room more than thirty years.

Lewis stopped at the front of his desk, leafed through the papers in the *incoming* basket, looked up as Sheriff Czernak entered. The sheriff, a fat man with wide Slavic features and a complexion like bread crust, grunted as he eased himself into the chair under the calendar. He pushed a brown felt hat to the back of his head, exposing a bald dome.

Lewis said, 'Hi, John. How's the wife?' He dropped the papers back into the basket.

'Her sciatica's better this week,' said the sheriff. 'I came in to tell you to skip that burglary report in the basket. A city prowler picked up two punks with the stuff early this morning. We're sending 'em over to juvenile court.'

'They'll never learn,' said Lewis.

'Got one little chore for you,' said the sheriff. 'Otherwise everything's quiet. Maybe we'll get a chance to catch up on our paper work.' He hoisted himself out of the chair. 'Doc Bellarmine did the autopsy on that Cerino woman, but he left a bottle of stomach washings at the Johnson-Tule Mortuary. Could you pick up the bottle and run it out to the county hospital?'

'Sure,' said Lewis. 'But I'll bet her death was natural causes. She was a known alcoholic. All those bottles in her shack.'

'Prob'ly,' said the sheriff. He stopped in front of Lewis' desk, glanced up at the calendar art. 'Some dish.'

Lewis grinned. 'When I find a gal like that I'm going to get married,' he said.

'You do that,' said the sheriff. He ambled out of the office.

It was almost 8:30 when Lewis cruised past the mortuary in his county car and failed to find a parking place in the block. At the next corner, Cove Street, he turned right and went up the alley, parking on the concrete apron to the mortuary garage.

A southwest wind which had been threatening storm all night kicked up a damp gust as he stepped from the car. Lewis glanced up at the gray sky, but left his raincoat over the back of the seat. He went down the narrow walk beside the garage, found the back door of the mortuary ajar. Inside was a hallway and a row of three metal tanks, the tall kind welders use for oxygen and acetylene gas. Lewis glanced at them, wondered what a mortuary did with that type of equipment, shrugged the question aside. At the other end of the hall the door opened into a carpeted foyer which smelled of musky flowers. A door at the left bore a brass plate labeled OFFICE. Lewis crossed the foyer, entered the room.

Behind a glass-topped desk in the corner sat a tall blond individual type with clear Nordic features. An oak frame on the wall behind him held a colored photograph of Mount Lassen labeled PEACE on an embossed nameplate. An official burial form – partly filled in – was on the desk in front of the man. The left corner of the desk held a brass cup in which sat a metal ball. The ball emitted a hissing noise as Lewis approached and he breathed in the heavy floral scent of the foyer.

The man behind the desk got to his feet, put a pen across the burial form. Lewis recognized him – Johnson, half owner of the mortuary.

'May I help you?' asked the mortician.

Lewis explained his errand.

Johnson brought a small bottle from a desk drawer, passed it across to Lewis, then looked at the deputy with a puzzled frown. 'How'd you get in?' asked the mortician. 'I didn't hear the front door chimes.'

The deputy shoved the bottle into a side pocket of his coat. 'I parked in the alley and came in the back way,' he said. 'The street out front is full of Odd Fellows cars.'

'Odd Fellows?' Johnson came around the desk.

'Paper said they were having some kind of rummage sale today,' said Lewis. He ducked his head to look under the shade on the front window. 'I guess those are Odd Fellows cars. That's the hall across the street.'

An ornamental shrub on the mortuary front lawn bent before the wind and a spattering of rain drummed against the window. Lewis straightened. 'Left my raincoat in the car,' he said. 'I'll just duck out the way I came.'

Johnson moved to his office door. 'Two of our attendants are due back now on a call,' he said. 'They—'

'I've seen a stiff before,' said Lewis. He stepped past Johnson, headed for the door to the rear hall.

Johnson's hand caught the deputy's shoulder. 'I must insist you go out the front,' said the mortician.

Lewis stopped, his mind setting up a battery of questions. 'It's raining out,' he said. 'I'll get all wet.'

'I'm sorry,' said Johnson.

Another man might have shrugged and complied with Johnson's request, but Welby Lewis was the son of the late Proctor Lewis, who had been three times president of the Banbury County Sherlock Holmes Round Table. Welby had cut his teeth on *logical deduction* and the logic of this situation escaped him. He reviewed his memory of the hallway. Empty except for those tanks near the back door.

'What do you keep in those metal tanks?' he asked.

The mortician's hand tightened on his shoulder and Lewis felt himself turned toward the front door. 'Just embalming fluid,' said Johnson. 'That's the way it's delivered.'

'Oh.' Lewis looked up at Johnson's tightly drawn features, pulled away from the restraining hand and went out the front door. Rain was driving down and he ran around the side of the mortuary to his car, jumping in, slammed the door and sat down to wait. At 9:28am by his wrist watch an assistant mortician came out, opened the garage doors. Lewis leaned across the front seat, rolled down his right window.

'You'll have to move your car,' said the assistant. 'We're going out on a call.'

'When are the other fellows coming back?' asked Lewis.

The mortician stopped halfway inside the garage. 'What other fellows?' he asked.

'The ones who went out on that call this morning.'

'Must be some other mortuary,' said the assistant. 'This is our first call today.'

'Thanks,' said Lewis. He rolled up his window, started the car and drove to the county hospital. The battery of unanswered questions churned in his mind. Foremost was –

Why did Johnson lie to keep me from going out the back way?

At the hospital he delivered the bottle to the pathology lab, found a pay booth and called the Banbury Mortuary. An attendant answered and Lewis said, 'I want to settle a bet. Could you tell me how embalming fluid is delivered to mortuaries?'

'We buy it by the case in concentrated form,' said the mortician. 'Twenty-four glass bottles to the case, sixteen ounces to the bottle. It contains red or orange dye to give a lifelike appearance. Our particular brand smells somewhat like strawberry soda. There is nothing offensive about it. We guarantee that the lifelike—'

'I just wanted to know how it came,' said Lewis. 'You're sure it's never delivered in metal tanks?'

'Good heavens, no!' said the man. 'It'd corrode them!'

'Thanks,' said Lewis and hung up softly. In his mind was the Holmesian observation: *If a man lies about an apparently inconsequential thing, then that thing is not inconsequential.*

He stepped out of the booth and bumped into Dr Bellarmine, the autopsy surgeon. The doctor was a tall, knobby character with gray hair, sun-lamp tan and blue eyes as cutting as two scalpels.

'Oh, there you are, Lewis,' he said. 'They told me you were down this way. We found enough alcohol in that Cerino woman to kill three people. We'll check the stomach washings, too, but I doubt they'll add anything.'

'Cerino woman?' asked Lewis.

'The old alcoholic you found in that shack by the roundhouse,' said Bellarmine. 'You losing your memory?'

'Oh . . . oh, certainly,' said Lewis. 'I was just thinking of something else. Thanks, Doc.' He brushed past the surgeon. 'Gotta go now,' he muttered.

Back at his office Lewis sat on a corner of his desk, pulled the telephone to him and dialed the Johnson-Tule Mortuary. An unfamiliar masculine voice answered. Lewis said, 'Do you do cremations at your mortuary?'

'Not *at* our mortuary,' said the masculine voice, 'but we have an arrangement with Rose Lawn Memorial Crematorium. Would you care to stop by and discuss your problem?'

'Not right now, thank you,' said Lewis, and replaced the phone on its hook. He checked off another question in his mind – the possibility that the tanks held gas for a crematorium. *What the devil's in those tanks?* he asked himself.

'Somebody die?' The voice came from the doorway, breaking into Lewis' reverie. The deputy turned, saw Sheriff Czernak.

'No,' said Lewis. 'I've just got a puzzle.' He went around the desk to his chair, sat down.

'Doc Bellarmine say anything about the Cerino dame?' asked the sheriff. He came into the room, eased himself into the chair beneath the calendar art.

'Alcoholism,' said Lewis. 'Like I said.' He leaned back in his chair, put his feet on the desk and stared at a stained spot on the ceiling.

'What's niggling you?' asked the sheriff. 'You look like a guy trying to solve a conundrum.'

'I am,' said Lewis and told him about the incident at the mortuary.

Czernak took off his hat, scratched his bald head. 'It don't sound like much to me, Welby. In all probability there's a very simple explanation.'

'I don't think so,' said Lewis.

'Why not?'

Lewis shook his head. 'I don't know. I just don't think so. Something about that mortuary doesn't ring true.'

'What you think's in them tanks?' asked the sheriff.

'I don't know,' said Lewis.

The sheriff seated his hat firmly on his head. 'Anybody else I'd tell 'em forget it,' he said. 'But you – I dunno. I seen you pull to many rabbits out of the hat. Sometimes I think you're a freak an' see inside people.'

'I am a freak,' said Lewis. He dropped his feet to the floor, pulled a scratch pad to him and began doodling.

'Yeah, I can see you got six heads,' said the sheriff.

'No, really,' said Lewis. 'My heart's on the right side of my chest.'

'I hadn't noticed,' said the sheriff. 'But now you point it out to me—'

'Freak,' said Lewis. 'That's what I felt looking at that mortician. Like he was some kind of a creepy freak.'

He pushed the scratch pad away from him. It bore a square broken into tiny segments by zigzag lines. Like a jigsaw puzzle.

'Was he a freak?'

Lewis shook his head. 'Not that I could see.'

Czernak pushed himself out of his chair. 'Tell you what,' he said. 'It's quiet today. Why'ncha nose around a little?'

'Who can I have to help me?' asked Lewis.

'Barney Keeler'll be back in about a half hour,' said Czernak. 'He's deliverin' a subpoena for Judge Gordon.'

'OK,' said Lewis. 'When he gets back tell him to go over to the Odd Fellows Hall and go in the back way without attracting too much attention. I want him to go up to that tower room and keep watch on the front of the mortuary, note down everybody who enters or leaves and watch for those tanks. If the tanks go out, he's to tail the carrier and find out where they go.'

'What're you gonna do?' asked the sheriff.

'Find a place where I can keep my eye on the back entrance. I'll call in when I get set.' Lewis hooked a thumb toward the desk across from his. 'When Joe Welch comes on, send him over to spell me.'

'Right,' said Czernak. 'I still think maybe you're coon-doggin' it up an empty tree.'

'Maybe I am,' said Lewis. 'But something shady about a mortuary gives my imagination the jumps. I keep thinking of how easy it could be for a mortician to get rid of an inconvenient corpse.'

'Stuff it in one of them tanks, maybe?' asked the sheriff.

'No. They weren't big enough.' Lewis shook his head. 'I just don't like the idea of the guy lying to me.'

It was shortly after 10:30am when Lewis found what he needed – a doctor's office in the rear of a building across the alley and two doors up from the mortuary garage. The doctor had three examining rooms on the third floor, the rear room looking down on the mortuary back yard. Lewis swore the doctor and his nurse to secrecy, set himself up in the back room with a pair of field glasses.

At noon he sent the nurse out for a hamburger and glass of milk for his lunch, had her watch the mortuary yard while he called his office and told the day radio operator where he was.

The doctor came into the back room at five o'clock, gave Lewis an extra set of keys for the office, asked him to be certain the door was locked when he left. Again Lewis warned the doctor against saying anything about the watch on the mortuary, stared the man down when it appeared he was about to ask questions. The doctor turned, left the room. Presently, a door closed solidly. The office was silent.

At about 7:30 it became too dark to distinguish clearly anything that might happen in the mortuary back yard. Lewis considered moving to a position in the alley, but two floodlights above the yard suddenly flashed on and the amber glow of a night light came from the window in the back door.

Joe Welch pounded on the door of the doctor's office at 8:20. Lewis admitted him, hurried back to the window with Welch following. The other deputy was a tall, nervous chain-smoker with a perpetual squint, a voice like a bassoon. He moved to a position beside Lewis at the window, said, 'What's doing? Sheriff John said something about some acetylene tanks.'

'It may be nothing at all,' said Lewis. 'But I've a feeling we're onto something big.' In a few short sentences he explained about his encounter with the mortician that morning.

'Don't sound exciting to me,' said Welch. 'What you expecting to find in those tanks?'

'I wish I knew,' said Lewis.

Welch went into the corner of the darkened room, lighted a cigarette, returned. 'Why don't you just ask this Johnson?'

'That's the point,' said Lewis. 'I did ask him and he lied to me. That's why I'm suspicious. I've been hoping they'd take those tanks out and we could trail them to wherever they go. Get our answer that way.'

'Why're you so sure it's the tanks he didn't want you to see?' asked Welch.

'That was a funny hallway,' said Lewis. 'Door at each end, none along the sides. Only things in it were those tanks.'

'Well, those tanks might already be gone,' said Welch. 'You didn't get on this end until about 10:30 you said and Keeler wasn't on the front until about eleven. They could've been taken out then if they're so all-fired important.'

'I've had the same thought,' said Lewis. 'But I don't think they have. I'm going out to grab a bite to eat now, then I'm going down in the alley for a closer look.'

'You won't get very close with all them lights on the yard,' said Welch.

Lewis pointed to the garage. 'If you look close you can see a space along the other side; in the shadow there. The light's on in the back hall. I'll try to get close enough for a look through the window in that rear door. They're tall tanks. I should be able to see them.'

'And if they've been moved some place else in the building?' asked Welch.

'Then I'll have to go in and brace Johnson for a showdown,' said Lewis. 'Maybe I should've done that in the first place, but this is a screwy situation. I just don't like a mystery in a mortuary.'

'Sounds like the title of a detective story,' said Welch. ' "Mystery In a Mortuary." '

Welch sniffed. 'There's already death inside there,' he said. 'This could be something mighty unpleasant.'

Welch lighted a new cigarette from the coal of the one he had been smoking, stubbed out the discard in a dish Lewis had been using for an ash tray. 'You may be right,' said Welch. 'The only thing impresses me about this she-bang, Welby, is like Sheriff John said – I've seen you pull too many rabbits out of the hat.'

'That's what he told you?' asked Lewis.

'Yeah, but he thinks maybe you're gonna pull a blank this time.' Welch stared down at the mortuary. 'If you go inside, do you want me to round up a few of my men and smother the place if you don't come out by some set time?'

'I don't think that'll be necessary,' said Lewis. 'Don't take any action unless you see something suspicious.'

Welch nodded his head. 'OK,' he said. He looked at the glowing tip of his cigarette, glanced down at the yard they were watching. 'Mortuaries give me the creeps anyway,' he said.

Lewis bolted a hot beef sandwich at a cafe two blocks from the mortuary, returned along a back street. It was cold and wet in the alley. A perverse wind kept tangling the skirts of his raincoat. He hugged the shadows near the mortuary garage, found the row of boards which had been nailed across the area he was going to use. Lewis clambered over the boards, dropped to soft earth which was out of the wind but under a steady dripping from unguttered eaves. He moved quietly to the end of the shadow area and, as he had expected, could see inside the window on the rear door of the mortuary. The tanks were not visible. Lewis cursed under his breath, shrugged, stepped out of the shadows and crossed the lighted back yard. The door was locked, but he could see through the window that the hallway was empty. He went around to the front door, rang the night bell.

A man in a rumpled black suit which looked as though

he had slept in it answered the door. Lewis brushed past him into the warm flower smell of the foyer. 'Is Johnson here?' he asked.

'Mr Johnson is asleep,' said the man. 'May I be of service?'

'Ask Mr Johnson to come down, please,' said Lewis. 'This is official business.' He showed his badge.

'Of course,' said the man. 'If you'll go into the office there and have a seat, I'll tell Mr Johnson you're here. He sleeps in the quarters upstairs.'

'Thanks,' said Lewis. He went into the office, looked at the colored photograph of Mount Lassen until the night attendant had disappeared up the stairs at the other end of the foyer. Then Lewis came out of the office, went to the doorway leading into the hall. The door was locked. He tried forcing it, but it wouldn't budge. He moved to the hinge side, found a thin crack which gave a view of the other end of the hall. What he saw made him draw in a quick breath. The three metal tanks were right where he had expected them to be. He went back to the office, found a directory and looked up the number of the doctor's office where Welch was waiting, dialed the number. After a long wait Welch's voice came on the line, tones guarded. 'Yes?'

'This is Welby,' said Lewis. 'Anything come in the back?'

'No,' said Welch. 'You all right?'

'I'm beginning to wonder,' said Lewis. 'Keep your eyes peeled.' He hung up, turned to find Johnson's tall figure filling the office doorway.

'Mr Lewis,' said Johnson. 'Is something wrong?' He came into the office.

'I want to have a look at those metal tanks,' said Lewis. Johnson stopped. 'What metal tanks?'

'The ones in your back hall,' said Lewis.

'Oh, the embalming fluid,' said Johnson. 'What's the interest in embalming fluid?'

'Let's just have a look at it,' said Lewis.

'Do you have a warrant?' asked Johnson.

Lewis' chin jerked up and he stared at the man. 'I wouldn't have a bit of trouble getting one,' he said.

'On what grounds?'

'I could think of something that'd stick,' said Lewis. 'Are we going to do this the easy way or the hard way?'

Johnson shrugged. 'As you wish.' He led the way out of the office, unlocked the hall door, preceded Lewis down the hallway to the three tanks.

'I thought embalming fluid came in sixteen-ounce glass bottles,' said Lewis.

'This is something new,' said Johnson. 'These tanks have glass inner liners. The fluid is kept under pressure.' He turned a valve and an acrid spray emerged from a fitting at the top.

Lewis took a shot in the dark, said, 'That doesn't smell like embalming fluid.'

Johnson said, 'It's a new type. We add the masking perfumes later.'

'You just get these filled?' asked Lewis.

'No, these were delivered last week,' said Johnson. 'We've left them here because we don't have a better place to store them.' He smiled at Lewis, but the eyes remained cold, watchful. 'Why this interest?'

'Call it professional curiosity,' said Lewis. He went to the rear door, unlatched it and locked the latch in the open position, stepped outside, closed the door. He could see the tanks plainly through the window. He came back into the hallway.

He's still lying to me, thought Lewis. *But it's all so very plausible.* He said, 'I'm going to give your place a thorough search.'

'But why?' protested Johnson.

'For no good reason at all,' said Lewis. 'If you want, I'll go out and get a warrant.' He started to brush past Johnson, was stopped by a strong hand on his shoulder, something hard pressing into his side. He looked down, saw a flat automatic menacing him.

'I regret this,' said Johnson. 'Believe me, I do.'

'You're going to regret it more,' said Lewis. 'I have your place watched front and back and the office knows where I am.'

For the first time he saw a look of indecision on Johnson's face. 'You're lying,' said the mortician.

'Come here,' said Lewis. He stepped to the back door, looked up to the black window where Welch stood. The glow of the deputy's cigarette was plainly visible, an orange wash against the blackness. Johnson saw it. 'Now let's go check the front,' said Lewis.

'No need,' said Johnson. 'I thought you were playing a lone hand.' He paused. 'You came in the back yard again and had a look in the window, didn't you?'

'What do you think?' asked Lewis.

'I should've anticipated that,' said Johnson. 'Perhaps I was too anxious to have things appear just as they were. You startled me coming in here at night like this.'

'You saw me come in the front?' asked Lewis.

'Let us say that I was aware you were downstairs before the attendant told me,' said Johnson. He gestured with his gun. 'Let's go back to the office.'

Lewis led the way down the hall. At the foyer door he glanced back.

'Turn around!' barked Johnson.

But the one glance had been enough. The tanks were gone. 'What was that humming sound?' asked Lewis.

'Just keep moving,' said Johnson.

In the front office, the mortician motioned Lewis to a chair. 'What were you looking for?' asked Johnson. He slid into the chair behind his desk, rested his gun hand on the desk top.

'I found what I was looking for,' said Lewis.

'And that is?'

'Evidence to confirm my belief that this place should be taken apart brick by brick.'

Johnson smiled, hooked the telephone to him with his

left hand, took off the receiver and rested it on the desk. 'What's your office number?'

Lewis told him.

Johnson dialed, picked up the phone, said, 'Hello, this is Lewis.'

Lewis came half out of the chair. His own voice was issuing from Johnson's mouth. The gun in the mortician's hand waved him back to the chair.

'You got the dope on what I'm doing?' asked Johnson. He waited. 'No. Nothing important. I'm just looking.' Again he paused. 'I'll tell you if I find anything,' he said. He replaced the phone in its cradle.

'Well?' said Lewis.

Johnson's lips thinned. 'This is incredible,' he said. 'A mere human—' He broke off, stared at Lewis, said, 'My mistake was in telling you a plausible lie after that door was left open. I should have—' He shrugged.

'You couldn't hope to fool us forever,' said Lewis.

'I suppose not,' said Johnson, 'but reasoning tells me that there is still a chance.' The gun suddenly came up, its muzzle pointing at Lewis. 'It's a chance I have to take,' said the mortician. The gun belched flame and Lewis was slammed back in his chair. Through a dimming haze, he saw Johnson put the gun to his own head, pull the trigger, slump across the desk. Then the haze around Lewis thickened, became the black nothing of unconsciousness.

From a somewhere he could not identify Lewis became aware of himself. He was running through a black cave, chased by a monster with blazing eyes and arms like an octopus. The monster kept shouting, 'A mere human! A mere human! A mere human!' with a voice that echoed as though projected into a rain barrel. Then, above the voice of the monster, Lewis heard water dripping in a quick even cadence. At the same time he saw the mouth of the cave, a round bright area. The bright area grew larger, larger, became the white wall of a hospital room and a window with sunshine outside. Lewis turned his head, saw a metal tank like the ones in the mortuary.

A voice said, 'That brought him around.'

Vertigo swept over Lewis and for a moment he fought it. A white clad figure swam into his field of vision, resolved itself into a county hospital intern whom Lewis recognized. The intern held a black oxygen mask.

The sound of the dripping water was louder now and then he realized that it was a wrist watch. He turned toward the sound, saw Sheriff Czernak straighten from a position close to his head. Czernak's Slavic face broke into a grin. 'Boy, you gave us a scare,' he said.

Lewis swallowed, found his voice. 'What—'

'You know, you are lucky you're a freak,' said Czernak. 'Your heart being on the right side's the only thing saved you. That and the fact that Joe heard the shots.'

The intern came around beside the sheriff. 'The bullet nicked an edge of your lung and took a little piece out of a rib at the back,' said the intern. 'You must've been born lucky.'

'Johnson?' said Lewis.

'Deader'n a mackerel,' said Czernak. 'You feel strong enough to tell us what happened? Joe's story don't make sense. What's with these tanks of embalming fluid?'

Lewis thought about his encounter with the mortician. Nothing about it made sense. He said, 'Embalming fluid comes in sixteen-ounce bottles.'

'We got those three tanks from the hallway,' said Czernak, 'but I don't know what we're doing with them.'

'From the hall?' Lewis remembered his last look at the empty hall before Johnson had ordered him to turn around. He tried to push himself up, felt pain knife through his chest. The intern pushed him gently back to the pillow. 'Here now, none of that,' he said. 'You just stay flat on your back.'

'What was in the tanks?' whispered Lewis.

'The lab here says it's embalming fluid,' said the sheriff. 'What's so special about it?'

Lewis remembered the acrid odor of the spray Johnson

had released from the tank valve. 'Does the lab still have some of that fluid?' he asked. 'I'd like to smell it.'

'I'll get it,' said the intern. 'Don't let him sit up. It could start a hemorrhage.' He went out the door.

'Where were the tanks when you found them?' asked Lewis.

'Down by the back door,' said Czernak. 'Where you said they were. Why?'

'I don't really know yet,' said Lewis. 'But I've something I wish you'd do. Take a—'

The door opened and the intern entered, a test tube in his hand. 'This is the stuff,' he said. He passed the tube under Lewis' nose. It gave off a musklike sweet aroma. It was not what he had smelled at the tanks. *That explains why the tanks disappeared,* he thought. *Somebody switched them. But what was in the others?* He looked up at the intern, said, 'Thanks.'

'You were sayin' something,' said the sheriff.

'Yes,' said Lewis. 'Take a crew over to that mortuary, John, and rip out the wall behind where you found those tanks and take up the floor under that spot.'

'What're we supposed to find?' asked Czernak.

'Damned if I know,' said Lewis, 'but it sure should be interesting. Those tanks kept disappearing and reappearing every time I turned my back. I want to know why.'

'Look, Welby, we've got to have something solid to go on,' said the sheriff. 'People are running around that mortuary like crazy, saying it's bad for business an' what all.'

'I'd say this was good for business,' said Lewis, a brief smile forming on his lips. His face sobered. 'Don't you think it's enough that somebody tried to kill one of your men and then committed suicide?'

The sheriff scratched his head. 'I guess so, Welby. You sure you can't give me anything more'n just your hunch?'

'You know as much about this as I do,' said Lewis. 'By the way, where's Johnson's body?'

'They're fixin' it up for burial,' said Czernak. 'Welby, I

really should have more'n just your say so. The DA will scream if I get too heavy handed.'

'You're still the sheriff,' said Lewis.

'Well, can't you even tell me why Johnson killed himself?'

'Say he was mentally unbalanced,' said Lewis. 'And John, here's something else. Get Doc Bellarmine to do the autopsy on Johnson and tell him to go over that body with a magnifying glass.'

'Why?'

'It was something he said about mere humans,' said Lewis.

'Askin' me to stick my neck out like this,' said Czernak.

'Will you do it?' asked Lewis.

'Sure I'll do it!' exploded Czernak. 'But I don't like it!' He jammed his hat onto his head, strode out of the room.

The intern turned to follow.

Lewis said, 'What time is it?'

The intern stopped, glanced at his wrist watch. 'Almost five.' He looked at Lewis. 'We've had you under sedatives since you came out of the operating room.'

'Five am or five pm?' asked Lewis.

'Five pm,' said the intern.

'Was I a tough job?' asked Lewis.

'It was a clean wound,' said the intern. 'You take it easy now. It's almost chow time. I'll see that you're served in the first round and then I'll have the nurse bring you a sedative. You need your rest.'

'How long am I going to be chained to this bed?' asked Lewis.

'We'll discuss that later,' said the intern. 'You really shouldn't be talking.' He turned away, went out the door.

Lewis turned his head away, saw that someone had left a stack of magazines on his bed stand. The top magazine had slipped down, exposing the cover. It was done in garish colors – a bug-eyed monster chasing a scantily clad female. Lewis was reminded of his nightmare. *A mere human . . . A mere human . . . A mere human.* The words kept turning over in his mind. *What was it about Johnson that brought up the idea of a freak?* he wondered.

A student nurse brought in his tray, cranked up his bed and helped him eat. Presently, a nurse came in with a hypo, shot him in the arm. He drifted off to sleep with the mind full of questions still unanswered.

'He's awake now,' said a female voice. Lewis heard a door open, looked up to see Czernak followed by Joe Welch. It was daylight outside, raining. The two men wore damp raincoats which they took off and draped over chairs.

Lewis smiled at Welch. 'Thanks for having good ears, Joe,' he said.

Welch grinned. 'I opened the window when I saw you come out the back door,' he said. 'I thought maybe you was going to holler something up to me. Then when you went right back inside, I thought that was funny; so I left the window partly open or I'd never've heard a thing.'

Czernak pulled a chair up beside Lewis' bed, sat down. Welch took a chair at the foot.

Lewis turned his head toward the sheriff. 'Is the DA screaming yet?'

'No,' said Czernak. 'He got caught out in that rainstorm the other day and he's home with the flu. Besides, I'm still sheriff of this county.' He patted the bed. 'How you feeling, boy?'

'I'm afraid I'm gonna live,' said Lewis.

'You better,' said Welch. 'We got a new relief radio gal who saw your picture in the files an' says she wants to meet you. She's a wow.'

'Tell her to wait for me,' said Lewis. He looked at the sheriff. 'What'd you find?'

'I don't get it, Welby,' said Czernak. 'Right behind where them tanks was there was this brick wall covered with plaster. We took away the plaster and there's all these wires, see.'

'What kind of wires?'

'That's just it, Keeler's old man is a jeweler and Keeler

says this wire is silver. It's kind of a screen like, criss-crossed every which way.'

'What were they hooked up to?'

'To nothing we could find,' said Czernak. He looked at Welch. 'Ain't that right?'

'Nothing there but this wire,' said Welch.

'What did you do with it?' asked Lewis.

'Nothing,' said Czernak. 'We just left it like it was and took pictures.'

'Anything under the floor?'

Czernak's face brightened. 'Boy, we sure hit the jackpot there!' He bent his head and peered closely at Lewis. 'How'd you know we'd find something under there?'

'I just knew those tanks kept appearing out of nowhere,' said Lewis. 'What was under there?'

Czernak straightened. 'Well, a whole section of the hall floor was an elevator and down below there was this big room. It stretched from under the hall to clear under the embalming room and there was a section of the embalming room floor where a bunch of tiles come up in one piece and there was a trapdoor and a stairway. Hell! It was just like one of them horror movies!'

'What was down there?'

'A buncha machinery,' said Czernak.

'What kind?'

'I dunno.' Czernak shook his head, glanced at Welch.

'Craziest stuff I ever saw,' said Welch. He shrugged.

'Doc Bellarmine came down and had a look at it after the autopsy last night,' said Czernak. 'He said he'd be in to see you this morning.'

'Did he saw anything about the autopsy?' asked Lewis.

'Not to me,' said Czernak.

Welch hitched his chair closer to the foot of the bed, rested an arm on the rail. 'He told me it was something about the autopsy made him come down to have a look at the mortuary,' he said. 'He didn't say what it was, though.'

'What about the mortuary staff?' asked Lewis. 'Did they say anything about the secret room?'

'They swear they never even knew it was there,' said Czernak. 'We took 'em all into custody anyway, all except Tule and his wife.'

'Tule?'

'Yeah, the other partner. His wife was a licensed mortician, too. Ain't been seen since the night you were shot. The staff says that Johnson, Tule and the wife was always locking doors around the building for no good reason at all.'

'What did this machinery look like?'

'Part of it was just an elevator for that section of floor. The other stuff was hooked up to a bunch of pipes coming down from the embalming table upstairs. There was this big—' Czernak stopped as the door opened.

Dr Bellarmine's cynical face peered into the room. His eyes swept over the occupants, he entered, closed the door behind him. 'The patient's feeling better, I see,' he said. 'For a while there I thought this would be a job for me in my official capacity.'

'This guy'll outlive all of us,' said Welch.

'He probably will at that,' said the doctor. He glanced down at Lewis. 'Feel like a little conversation?'

'Just a minute, Doc,' said Lewis. He turned to Czernak. 'John, I have one more favor,' he said. 'Could you get one of those tanks of embalming fluid to a welding shop and have it cut open with a burner. I want to know how it's made inside.'

'No you don't,' said Czernak. 'I'm not leavin' here without some kind of an explanation.'

'And I don't have an explanation,' said Lewis. 'All the pieces aren't together yet. I'm tied to this bed when I should be out working on this thing. I've ten thousand questions I want answered and no way of answering them.'

'Don't excite yourself,' said Bellarmine.

'Yeah, Welby, take it easy,' said Czernak. 'It's just that I'm about ready to pop with frustration. Nothing makes sense here. This guy tries to kill you for no apparent reason and then commits suicide. It seems to be because you wanted to look inside them tanks, but they're just embalming fluid. I don't get it.'

'Would you have those tanks cut open for me?' asked Lewis.

'OK, OK.' Czernak hoisted himself to his feet. Welch also arose. 'Come on, Joe,' said the sheriff. 'We're nothin' but a couple of leg men for Sherlock here. Let's take them—'

'John, I'm sorry,' said Lewis. 'It's just that I can't—'

'I know you can't do it yourself now,' said Czernak. 'That's why I'm doing it. You're the best man I got, Welby; so I'm countin' on you to put this together. Me, I gave up when I saw that machinery.' He left the room, muttering, followed by Welch, who stopped at the door, winked at Lewis.

Bellarmine waited until the door closed, sat down on the foot of the bed. 'How'd you get onto them?' he asked.

Lewis ignored the question. 'What'd you find in that autopsy?' he asked.

The surgeon frowned. 'I thought you were nuts when the sheriff told me what you wanted,' he said. 'Any fool could see Johnson died of a gunshot wound in the head. But I guess you had a reason; so I did my cutting carefully and it was a lucky thing I did.'

'Why?'

'Well, this is the kind of case an autopsy surgeon sloughs off sometimes. Visible wound. Obvious cause. I could've missed it. The guy looked to be normal.'

'Missed what?'

'His heart for one thing. It had an extra layer of muscles in the cardiac sheath. I experimented with them and near dropped my knife. They work like that automatic sealing device they put in airplane fuel tanks. Puncture the heart and this muscle layer seals the hole until the heart's healed.'

'Damn!' said Lewis.

'This guy was like that all over,' said Bellarmine. 'For a long time doctors have looked at the human body with

the wish they could redesign certain things to better speci-
fications. Johnson looked like our wish had come true.
Fewer vertebrae with better articulation. Pigment veins into
the pupil of the eye which could only be some kind of filter
to—'

'That's it!' Lewis slapped the bed with the palm of his
hand. 'There was something freakish about him and I
couldn't focus on it. The pupils of his eyes changed color.
I can remember seeing it and—'

'You didn't see anything,' said Bellarmine. 'His pelvic
floor was broader and distributed the weight more evenly
to the legs. The feet had larger bones and more central
distribution of weight over the arch. There was an inter-
laced membranous support for the viscera. His circulatory
system had sphincter valves at strategic points to control
bleeding. This Johnson may have looked human on the
outside, but inside he was superhuman.'

'What about that machinery in the mortuary basement?'
asked Lewis.

Bellarmine stood up, began to pace the floor, back and
forth at the foot of the bed. Presently, he stopped, put his
hands on the rail, stared at Lewis. 'I spent half the night
examining that layout,' he said. 'It was one of the most
beautifully designed and executed rigs I've ever seen. Its
major purpose was to take cadaver blood and fractionate
the protein.'

'You mean like for making plasma and stuff like that?'
asked Lewis.

'Well, something like that,' said Bellarmine.

'I didn't think you could use the blood of a corpse for
that,' said Lewis.

'We didn't either,' said the surgeon. 'The Russians have
been working on it, however. Our experience has been that
it breaks down too quickly. We've tried—'

'You mean this was a Communist setup?'

Bellarmine shook his head. 'No such luck. This rig
wasn't just foreign to the USA. It was foreign to Earth.
There's one centrifugal pump in there that spins free in an

air blast. I shudder every time I think of the force it must generate. We don't have an alloy that'll come anywhere near standing up to those strains. And the Russians don't have it, either.'

'How can you be sure?'

'For one thing, there are several research projects that are awaiting this type of rig and the Russians have no more results on those projects than we have.'

'Then something was produced from cadaver blood and was stored in those tanks,' said Lewis.

Bellarmine nodded. 'I checked. A fitting on the tanks matched one on the machinery.'

Lewis pushed himself upright, ignoring the pain in his chest. 'Then this means an extraterrestrial in—' The pain in his chest became too much and he sagged back to the pillow.

Dr Bellarmine was suddenly at his side. 'You fool!' he barked. 'You were told to take it easy.' He pushed the emergency button at the head of the bed, began working on the bandages.

'What's matter?' whispered Lewis.

'Hemorrhage,' said Bellarmine. 'Where's that fool nurse? Why doesn't she answer the bell?' He stripped away a length of adhesive.

The door opened and a nurse entered, stopped as she saw the scene.

'Emergency tray,' said Bellarmine. 'Get Dr Edwards here to assist! Bring plasma!'

Lewis heard a drum begin to pound inside his head – louder, louder, louder. Then it began to fade and there was nothing.

He awoke to a rustling sound and footsteps. Then he recognized it. The sound of a nurse's starched uniform as she moved about the room. He opened his eyes and saw by the shadows outside that it was afternoon.

'So you're awake,' said the nurse.

Lewis turned his head toward the sound. 'You're new,' he said. 'I don't recognize you.'

'Special,' she said. 'Now you just take it easy and don't try to move.' She pushed the call button.

It seemed that almost immediately Dr Bellarmine was in the room bending over Lewis. The surgeon felt Lewis' wrist, took a deep breath. 'You went into shock,' he said. 'You have to remain quiet. Don't try to move around.'

His voice low and husky, Lewis said, 'Could I ask some questions?'

'Yes, but only for a few minutes. You have to avoid any kind of exertion.'

'What'd the sheriff find out about the tanks?'

Bellarmine grimaced. 'They couldn't open them. Can't cut the metal.'

'That confirms it,' said Lewis. 'Think there are any other rigs like that?'

'There have to be,' said Bellarmine. He sat down on a chair at the head of the bed. 'I've had another look at that basement layout and took a machinist with me. He agrees. Everything about it cries out mass production. Mostly cast fittings with a minimum of machining. Simple, efficient construction.'

'Why? What good's the blood from human cadavers?'

'I've been asking myself that same question,' said Bellarmine. 'Maybe for a nutrient solution for culture growths. Maybe for the antibodies.'

'Would they be any good?'

'That depends on how soon the blood was extracted. The time element varies with temperature, body condition, a whole barrel full of things.'

'But why?'

The surgeon ran a hand through his gray hair. 'I don't like my answer to that question,' he said. 'I keep thinking of how we fractionate the blood of guinea pigs, how we recover vaccine from chick embryos, how we use all of our test animals.'

Lewis' eyes fell on the dresser across his room. Someone

had taken the books from his night stand and put them on the dresser. He could still see the bug-eyed monster cover.

'From what I know of science fiction,' said Lewis, 'that silver grid in the hall must be some kind of matter transmitter for sending the tanks to wherever they're used. I wonder why they didn't put it downstairs with the machinery.'

'Maybe it had to be above ground,' said Bellarmine. 'You figure it the same way I do.'

'You're a hard-headed guy, Doc,' said Lewis. 'How come you go for this bug-eyed monster theory?'

'It was the combination,' said Bellarmine. 'That silver grid, the design of the machinery and its purpose, the strange metals, the differences in Johnson. It all spells A-L-I-E-N, alien. But I could say the same holds for you, Lewis. What put you wise?'

'Johnson. He called me a *mere human*. I got to wondering how alien a guy could be to separate himself from the human race.'

'It checks,' said Bellarmine.

'But why guinea pigs?' asked Lewis.

The surgeon frowned, looked at the floor, back at Lewis. 'That rig had a secondary stage,' he said. 'It could have only one function – passing live virus under some kind of bombardment – X-ray or beta ray or whatever – and depositing the mutated strain in a little spray container about as big as your fist. I know from my own research experience that some mutated virus can be deadly.'

'Germ warfare,' whispered Lewis. 'You sure it isn't the Russians?'

'I'm sure. This was a perfect infecting center. Complete. Banbury would've been decimated by now if that's what it was.'

'Maybe they weren't ready.'

'Germ warfare is ready when one infecting center is set up. No. This rig was for producing slight alterations in common germs or I miss my guess. This little spray container went into a . . .'

'Rack on Johnson's desk,' said Lewis.

'Yeah,' said Bellarmine.

'I saw it,' said Lewis. 'I thought it was one of those deodorant things.' He picked a piece of lint off the covers. 'So they're infecting us with mutated virus.'

'It scares me,' said Bellarmine.

Lewis squinted his eyes, looked up at the surgeon, 'Doc, what would you do if you found out that one of your white rats was not only intelligent but had found out what you were doing to it?'

'Well –' Bellarmine looked out the window at the gathering dusk. 'I'm no monster, Lewis. I'd probably turn it loose. No—' He scratched his chin. 'No, maybe I wouldn't at that. But I wouldn't infect it anymore. I think I'd put it through some tests to find out just how smart it was. The rat would no longer be a simple test animal. Its usefulness would be in the psychological field, to tell me things about myself.'

'That's about the way I had it figured,' said Lewis. 'How much longer am I going to be in this bed?'

'Why?'

'I've figured a way for the guinea pigs to tell the researchers the jig's up.'

'How? We don't even know their language. We've only seen one specimen and that one's dead. We can't be sure they'd react the same way we would.'

'Yes they would,' said Lewis.

'How can you say that? They must already know we're sentient.'

'So's a rat sentient – to a degree,' said Lewis. 'It's all in the way you look at it. Sure. Compared to us, they're vegetables. That's the way it'd be with—'

'We don't have the right to take risks with the rest of humanity,' protested Bellarmine. 'Man, one of them tried to kill you!'

'But everything points to that one being defective,' said Lewis. 'He made too many mistakes. That's the only reason we got wise to him.'

'They might dump us into the incinerator as no longer useful,' said Bellarmine. 'They—'

Lewis said, 'They'd have to be pretty much pure scientists. Johnson was a field man, a lab technician, a worker. The pure scientists would follow our human pattern. I'm sure of it. To be a pure scientist you have to be able to control yourself. That means you'd understand other persons' – other beings' – problems. No, Doc. Your first answer was the best one. You'd put your rats to psychological tests.'

Bellarmine stared at his hands. 'What's your idea?'

'Take a white rat in one of those little lab cages. Infect it with some common germ, leave the infecting hypo in the cage, put the whole works – rat and all – in front of that silver grid. Distort—'

'That's a crazy idea,' said Bellarmine. 'How could you tell a hypothetical something to look at your message when you don't even know the hypothetical language – how to contact them in the first place.'

'Distort the field of that grid by touching the wires with a piece of metal,' said Lewis. 'Tie the metal to the end of a pole for safety.'

'I've never heard a crazier idea,' said Bellarmine.

'Get me the white rat, the cage and the hypo and I'll do it myself,' said Lewis.

Bellarmine got to his feet, moved toward the door. 'You're not doing anything for a couple of weeks,' he said. 'You're a sick man and I've been talking to you too long already.' He opened the door, left the room.

Lewis stared at the ceiling. A shudder passed over his body. *Mutated virus!*

The door opened and an orderly and nurse entered. 'You get a little tube feeding of hot gelatin,' said the nurse. She helped him eat it, then, over his protests, gave him a sedative.

'Doctor's orders,' said the nurse.

Through a descending fog, Lewis murmured, 'Which doctor?'

'Dr Bellarmine,' she said.

The fog came lower, darkened. He drifted into a nightmare peopled by thousands of Johnsons, all of them running around with large metal tanks asking, 'Are you human?' and collecting blood.

Sheriff Czernak was beside the bed when Lewis awoke. Lewis could see out the window that dawn was breaking. He turned toward the sheriff. 'Mornin', John,' he whispered. His tongue felt thick and dry.

' 'Bout time you woke up,' said Czernak. 'I've been waiting here a coupla hours. Something fishy going on.'

'Wind my bed up, will you?' asked Lewis. 'What's happening?'

Czernak arose, moved to the foot of the bed and turned the crank.

'The big thing is that Doc Bellarmine has disappeared,' he said. 'We traced him from the lab here to the mortuary. Then he just goes *pffft!*'

Lewis' eyes widened. 'Was there a white rat cage?'

'There you go again!' barked Czernak. 'You tell me you don't know anything about this, but you sure know all the questions.' He bent over Lewis. 'Sure there was a rat cage! You better tell me how you knew it!'

'First tell *me* what happened,' said Lewis.

Czernak straightened, frowning. 'All right, Welby, but when I get through telling, then you better tell.' He wet his lips with his tongue. 'I'm told the Doc came in here and talked to you last night. Then he went down to the lab and got one of them white rats with its cage. Then he went over to the mortuary. He had the cage and rat with him. Our night guard let him in. After a while, when the Doc didn't come out, the guard got worried and went inside. There in the back hall is the Doc's black bag. And over where this silver wire stuff was he finds—'

'Was?' Lewis barked the word.

'Yeah,' said Czernak wearily. 'That's the other thing.

Sometime last night somebody ripped out all them wires and didn't leave a single trace.'

'What else did the guard find?'

Czernak ran a hand under his collar, stared at the opposite wall.

'Well?'

'Welby, look, I—'

'What happened?'

'Well, the night guard – it was Rasmussen – called me and I went right down. Rasmussen didn't touch a thing. There was the Doc's bag, a long wood pole with a tire iron attached to it and the rat cage. The rat was gone.'

'Was there anything in the cage?'

Czernak suddenly leaned forward, blurted, 'Look, Welby, about the cage. There's something screwy about it. When I first got there I swear it wasn't there. Rasmussen doesn't remember it either. My first idea when I got there was that the Doc'd gone out the back way, but our seal was still on the door. It hadn't been opened. While I was thinkin' that one over – I was standing about in the middle of the hall – I heard this noise like a cork being pulled out of a bottle. I turned around and there was this little cage on the floor. Out of nowhere.'

'And it was empty?'

'Except for some pieces of glass that I'm told belonged to a hypo.'

'Broken?'

'Smashed to pieces.'

'Was the cage door open?'

Czernak tipped his head to one side, looked at the far wall. 'No, I don't believe it was.'

'And exactly where was this cage?' Lewis' eyes burned into the sheriff's.

'Like I said, Welby. Right in front of where the wires was.'

'And the wires were gone?'

'Well—' Again the sheriff looked uncomfortable. 'For

just a second there when I turned around after hearing that noise – for just a second there I thought I saw 'em.'

Lewis took a deep breath.

Czernak said, 'Now come on and give, will you? Where's the Doc? You must have some idea, the way you been askin' questions.'

'He's taking his entrance exams,' said Lewis. 'And we'd all better pray that he passes.'

GAMBLING DEVICE

'Desert Rest Hotel – No Gambling'

The blue and white sign, scraggly alkali sedge clustering around its supports, stood by itself at the edge of the lonely road.

Hal Remsen read it aloud, stopped his convertible at the hotel drive and glanced down at his bride of six hours. The heavy floral scent of her corsage wafted up to him. He smiled, the action bringing his thin dark features into vivid aliveness.

Ruth Remsen's short blond hair had been tangled by the long drive in the open car. Her disarrayed hair, backlighted now by a crimson sunset, accented a piquant doll quality in her small features.

'Well?' he said.

'Hal, I don't like the looks of that place,' she said. Her eyes narrowed. 'It looks like a prison. Let's try farther on.'

She suddenly shivered, staring across her husband at the blocky structure nestled in dry sand hills to their left. The hotel's shadowed portico gaped like a trap at the end of the dark surfaced driveway.

Hal shrugged, grinned. It gave him the sudden look of a small boy about to admit who stole the cookies.

'I have a confession,' he said. 'Your husband, the irreplaceable trouble shooter of Fowler Electronics, Inc, is lost.' He hesitated. 'That left turn at Meridian . . .'

'I still don't like the looks of that place,' she said. Her face sobered. 'Darling, it's our wedding night.'

He turned away from her to look at the hotel.

'It's just the way the sunset's lighting it,' he said. 'It makes those windows look like big red eyes.'

Ruth chewed her lower lip, continued to stare at the building in the parched hills. Rays of the setting sun, reflected off mineral sands, painted red streaks across the structure, gleamed like fire on the windows and their metal frames.

'Well . . .' She allowed her voice to trail off.

Hal put the car in gear, turned into the drive.

'It'll be dark soon,' he said. 'There's no dusk on the desert. We'd better take this while we can.'

He stopped the car in the gloom of the portico.

An ancient bellboy with a leathery mask of a face, and wearing a green uniform, came down the two steps at their right. Yellow lobby lights pouring through the double doors behind him silhouetted his stick-like frame.

Without speaking, he opened the car door for Ruth.

Hal slid across the seat after her, nodded toward the rear. 'Those two bags on the seat,' he said. 'We'll just be staying the night.'

He left the keys in the car.

The lobby held a cool stillness after the desert's heat. The tapping of their heels echoed across the tile floor. Hal was struck by the curious absence of plants, furniture and people. The quiet held an eerie, waiting quality.

They crossed to a marble topped semi-circular desk at the far side. Hal pushed a call button on the desk. He heard a double click behind him, turned to see the bellboy putting down their luggage.

If he were a woman, they'd call him a 'crone', thought Hal. The word 'warlock' popped into his mind.

The man moved around behind the desk with a kind of slithering, shambling walk. He pushed register and pen toward Hal.

Ruth looked at the register, glanced at Hal.

Suddenly conscious of his newly married status, Hal cleared his throat.

'Do you have a suite?' he asked.

'You have room 417 in the northwest corner,' said the man.

'Is that all you have?' asked Hal. He glanced down at Ruth, took a deep breath to overcome an abrupt feeling of disquiet. He looked back at the man across the desk.

'That's your room, sir,' said the man. He touched the edge of the register.

'Oh, take it,' said Ruth. 'It's just for tonight.'

Hal shrugged, took up the pen, signed, 'Mr and Mrs Harold B. Remsen, Sonoma, California' with an overdone flourish.

The man took the pen from Hal, put it in the fold of the register. He came back around the desk, still with that peculiar shambling gait – an almost mechanical motion.

'This way, please,' he said, taking up the luggage.

They went diagonally across the lobby, into an elevator that hummed faintly as the bellboy closed the door, sent the machine upward.

Ruth took hold of Hal's arm, gripped it tightly. He patted her hand, feeling a tremor of skin as he touched her. He stared at the back of the bellboy's green uniform. Irregular radial wrinkles stretched downward from the neck. Hal coughed.

'We turned left on what we thought was Route 25 back there at Meridian,' he said. 'We're headed for Carson City.'

The bellboy remained silent.

'Was that a wrong turn?' asked Ruth. Her voice came out high pitched, strained.

'There is no such thing as a *wrong* turn,' said the bellboy. He spoke without turning, brought the elevator to a stop, opened the door, took up their bags. 'This way, please.'

Hal looked down at his bride. She raised her eyebrows, shrugged.

'A philosopher,' he whispered.

The hall seemed to stretch out endlessly, like a dark cave with a barred window at the end. Through the window they could see night sweeping suddenly over the desert, bright stars clustering along the horizon. A silvery glow shimmered from the corners of the ceiling, illuminating the soft maroon carpet underfoot.

At the end of the hall, the bellboy opened a door,

reached in, turned on a light. He stepped aside, waited for Hal and Ruth to enter.

Hal paused in the yellow light of the threshold, smiled down at his bride. He made a lifting motion with his hands. She blushed, shook her head, stepped firmly into the room. He chuckled, followed her into the room.

It was a low ceilinged oblong space. A double bed stood at the far end, a metal dresser to their right flanked by two partly open doors. Through one door they could see the tile gleam of a bathroom. The other door showed the empty darkness of a closet. The room gave an impression of cell-like austerity. Windows by the bed looked out on the purple of the desert night.

Ruth went to the dresser mirror, began unpinning her corsage. The bellboy put their bags on a stand near the bed. Hal could see Ruth watching the man in the mirror.

'What did you mean "no such thing as a *wrong* turn"?' she asked.

The bellboy straightened. His green uniform settled into a new pattern of wrinkles. 'All roads lead somewhere,' he said. He turned, headed for the door.

Hal brought his hand from his pocket with a tip. The man ignored him, marched out, closing the door behind him.

'Well, I'll be . . .'

'Hal!' Ruth put a hand to her mouth, staring at the door.

He jerked around, feeling the panic in her voice.

'There's no door handle on the inside!' she said.

He looked at the blank inner surface of the door. 'Probably a hidden button or an electric eye,' he said. He went to the door, felt its surface, explored the wall on both sides.

Ruth came up behind him, clutched his arm. He could feel her trembling.

'Hal, I'm deathly afraid,' she said. 'Let's get out of here and . . .'

From somewhere, a deep rumbling voice interrupted her. 'Please do not be alarmed.'

Hal straightened, turned, trying to locate the source of the voice. He could feel Ruth's fingernails biting into his arm.

'You are now residents of the Desert Rest Hotel,' said the voice. 'Your stay need not be unpleasant as long as you observe our one rule: No gambling. You will not be permitted to gamble in any way. All gambling devices will be removed if you attempt to disobey.'

'I want to leave here,' quavered Ruth.

The nightmare quality of the scene struck Hal. He seriously considered for a brief second that he might be dreaming. But there was too much reality here: Ruth trembling beside him, the solid door, the gray wall.

'Some crackpot fanatic,' he muttered.

'You may decide to leave,' said the voice, 'but you have no choice of where you will go, in what manner or when. Free choice beyond the immediate decision is a gamble. Here, nothing is left to chance. Here, you have the absolute security of pre-determination.'

'What the hell is this?' demanded Hal.

'You have heard the rule,' said the voice. 'You decided to come here. The die is cast.'

What have I gotten us into? wondered Hal. *I should have listened to Ruth when she wanted to go on.*

Ruth was trembling so sharply that she shook his arm; he fought down a panic of his own.

'Hal, let's get out of here,' she said.

'Careful,' he said. 'Something's very wrong.' He patted her hand with what he hoped was some reassurance. 'Let's ... go ... down ... to ... the ... lobby,' he said, spacing his words evenly. He squeezed her hand.

She took a shuddering breath. 'Yes, I want to go.'

And how are we going to do it? he wondered. *No handle on the door.* He looked to the windows and the night beyond them. *Four stories down.*

'You have decided to go to the lobby?' asked the voice.

'Yes,' said Hal.

'Your decision has been entered,' said the voice. 'Time was allotted when you entered.'

Time allotted, he thought. *Ruth had it pegged: A prison.*

'What's going to happen to us?' she asked. She turned, buried her face against him. 'Darling, don't let anything happen to us.'

He held her tightly, looking around the room.

The hall door swung inward.

'The door just opened,' he said. 'Be calm. Don't let go of my arm.'

He led the way out of the room and to the elevator. No operator in the elevator, but the door closed as soon as they entered. The car descended, came to a smooth stop; the door opened.

People!

The change in the lobby hit them as soon as they left the elevator.

The lobby thronged with people. Silent, watchful people – strolling singly, in couples, in groups.

'I saw you come in and decided at that moment to speak to you.' It was a woman's voice: old, quavering.

Hal and Ruth turned to their left toward the voice. The speaker was gray-haired with a narrow, seamed face. She wore a blue dress of old fashioned cut that hung loosely about her body as though she had withered away from it.

Hal tried to speak, found with sudden panic that he could not utter a sound.

'I imagine several of us made the same decision,' said the old woman. Her eyes glittered as she stared at them. 'This time fell to me.' She nodded. 'Presumably you will not be able to talk to me because you haven't placed a decision and it does seem somewhat chancey. No matter.'

She shook her gray head. 'I know your questions. You're strays by the look of you. Newlyweds, too, I'd guess. More's the pity.'

Again, Hal tried to speak, couldn't. He felt a strange

stillness in Ruth beside him. He looked down at her. Ruth's face had a strained, bloodless appearance.

'We can give you a pretty educated guess as to what this hotel is,' said the old woman. 'It's a kind of a hospital from some far off place. Why it's located here we don't know. But we're pretty certain of what it's supposed to do: it's supposed to cure the gambling habit.'

Again the old woman nodded as though at some inner thought.

'I had the habit myself,' she said. 'We think the hotel has an aura that attracts gamblers when they come within range. Sometimes it picks up strays like yourselves. But it's a machine and can't refine its selection. It considers the strangest things to be gambling!'

Hal remembered the rumbling voice in the room: 'No Gambling!'

Behind the woman, in the center of the lobby, a short man in a high necked collar and suit that had been fashionable in the mid-twenties abruptly clutched his throat. He fell to the floor without a sound, lay there like a mound of soiled laundry.

The nightmare feeling returned to Hal.

From somewhere, the ancient bellboy appeared on the scene, hurried across the lobby, dragged the fallen man from sight around a corner.

'Someone just died,' said the old woman. 'I can see it in your eyes. The time of your death is chosen the moment you enter this place. Even the way you'll die.' She shuddered. 'Some of the ways are not pleasant.'

Coldness clutched at Hal.

The old woman sighed. 'You'll want to know if there's hope of escape.' She shrugged. 'Perhaps. Some just disappear. But maybe that's another . . . way.'

With an abrupt wrenching sensation, Hal found his voice. It startled him so that all he could say was: 'I can speak.' His voice came out flat and expressionless. Then: 'There must be some choice.'

The old woman shook her head. 'No. The moment for

you to speak – alone or in company – was set when you came in that front door.'

Hal took two quick deep breaths, fought for the power to reason in spite of fear. He gripped Ruth's arm, not daring to look at her, not wanting the distraction. There had to be a way out of this place. An ace trouble shooter for an electronics instruments factory should be the one to find that way.

'What would happen if I tried to gamble?' he asked.

The old woman shuddered. 'The device you chose for gambling would be removed,' she said. 'That's the reason you two mustn't . . .' she hesitated '. . . sleep together.'

Hal took a coin from his pocket, flipped it into the air. 'Call it and it's yours,' he said.

The coin failed to come down.

'You're being shown the power of this place,' said the old woman. 'You mustn't gamble . . . the instrument of chance is always removed.'

An abrupt thought washed through Hal's mind. *Would it* . . . He wet his lips with his tongue, fought to keep his face expressionless. *It's crazy*, he thought. *But no crazier than this nightmare.*

Slowly, he took another coin from his pocket.

'My wife and I are going to gamble again,' he said. 'We are going to gamble, using the hotel *and* this coin as the gambling device. The moment of interference is the thing upon which we are gambling.'

He felt an intensification of the silence in the lobby, was extremely conscious of Ruth's fingers digging into his arm, the curious questioning look on the old woman's face.

'We are gambling upon the moment when the hotel will remove my coin or *if* it will remove my coin,' he said. 'We will make one of several decisions dependent upon the moment of interference or the lack of interference.'

A deep grinding rumble shook the hotel.

He flipped the coin.

Hal and Ruth found themselves standing alone on a sand dune, moonlight painting the desert a ghostly silver around them. They could see the dark shape of their car on another dune.

Ruth threw herself into his arms, clung to him, sobbing. He stroked her shoulder.

'I hope they all heard me,' he said. 'That hotel is a robot. It has to remove *itself* when it becomes a gambling device.'

LOOKING FOR SOMETHING?

Mirsar Wees, chief indoctrinator for Sol III sub-prefecture, was defying the intent of the Relaxation-room in his quarters. He buzzed furiously back and forth from metal wall to metal wall, his pedal-membrane making a cricket-like sound as the vacuum cups disengaged.

'The fools!' he thought. 'The stupid, incompetent, mindless fools!'

Mirsar Wees was a Denebian. His race had originated more than three million earth years ago on the fourth planet circling the star Deneb – a planet no longer existing. His profile was curiously similar to that of a tall woman in a floor-length dress, with the vacuum-cup pedal-membrane contacting the floor under the 'skirt.' His eight specialized extensors waved now in a typical Denebian rage-pattern. His mouth, a thin transverse slit entirely separate from the olfactory-lung orifice directly below it, spewed forth a multi-lingual stream of invective against the assistant who cowered before him.

'How did this happen?' he shouted. 'I take my first vacation in one hundred years and come back to find my career almost shattered by your incompetency!'

Mirsar Wees turned and buzzed back across the room. Through his vision-ring, an organ somewhat like a glittering white tricycle-tire jammed down about one-third of the distance over his head, he examined again the report on Earthling Paul Marcus and maintained a baleful stare upon his assistant behind him. Activating the vision cells at his left, he examined the wall chronometer.

'So little time,' he muttered. 'If only I had someone at Central Processing who could see a deviant when it comes by! Now I'll have to take care of this bumble myself, before it gets out of hand. If they hear of it back at the bureau . . .'

Mirsar Wees, the Denebian, a cog in the galaxy-wide korad-farming empire of his race, pivoted on his pedal-membrane and went out a door which opened soundlessly before him. The humans who saw his flame-like profile this night would keep alive the folk tales of ghosts, djinn, little people, fairies, elves, pixies . . .

Were they given the vision to see it, they would know also that an angry overseer had passed. But they would not see this, of course. That was part of Mirsar Wees' job.

It was mainly because Paul Marcus was a professional hypnotist that he obtained an aborted glimpse of the rulers of the world.

The night it happened he was inducing a post-hypnotic command into the mind of an audience-participant to his show on the stage of the Roxy Theater in Tacoma, Washington.

Paul was a tall, thin man with a wide head which appeared large because of this feature although it really was not. He wore a black tailcoat and formal trousers, jewelled cuff links and chalkwhite cuffs, which gleamed and flashed as he gestured. A red spotlight in the balcony gave a Mephisto cast to his stage-setting, which was dominated by a backdrop of satin black against which gleamed two giant, luminous eyes. He was billed as 'Marcus the Mystic' and he looked the part.

The subject was a blonde girl whom Paul had chosen because she displayed signs of a higher than ordinary intelligence, a general characteristic of persons who are easily hypnotized. The woman had a good figure and showed sufficient leg when she sat down on the chair to excite whistles and cat-calls from the front rows. She flushed, but maintained her composure.

'What is your name, please?' Paul asked.

She answered in a contralto voice, 'Madelyne Walker.'

'Miss or Mrs?'

She said, 'Miss.'

Paul held up his right hand. From it dangled a gold

chain on the end of which was a large paste gem with many facets cut into its surface. A spotlight in the wings was so directed that it reflected countless star-bursts from the gem.

'If you will look at the diamond,' Paul said. 'Just keep your eyes on it.'

He began to swing the gem rhythmically, like a pendulum, from side to side. The girl's eyes followed it. Paul waited, until her eyes were moving in rhythm with the swinging bauble before he began to recite in a slow monotone, timed to the pendulum:

'Sleep. You will fall asleep . . . deep sleep . . . deep sleep . . . asleep . . . deep asleep . . . asleep . . . asleep . . .'

Her eyes followed the gem.

'Your eyelids will become heavy,' Paul said. 'Sleep. Go to sleep. You are falling asleep . . . deep, restful sleep . . . healing sleep . . . deep asleep . . . asleep . . . asleep . . . asleep . . .'

Her head began to nod, eyelids to close and pop open, slower and slower. Paul gently moved his left hand up to the chain. In the same monotone he said, 'When the diamond stops swinging you will fall into a deep, restful sleep from which only I can awaken you.' He allowed the gem to swing slower and slower in shorter and shorter sweeps. Finally, he put both palms against the chain and rotated it. The bauble at the end of the chain began to whirl rapidly, its facets coruscating with the reflections of the spotlight.

Miss Walker's head fell forward and Paul kept her from falling off the chair by grasping her shoulder. She was in deep trance. He began demonstrating to the audience the classic symptoms which accompany this – insensitivity to pain, body rigidity, complete obedience to the hypnotist's voice.

The show went along in routine fashion. Miss Walker barked like a dog. She became the dowager queen with dignified mien. She refused to answer to her own name. She conducted the imaginary symphony orchestra. She sang an operatic aria.

The audience applauded at the correct places in the performance. Paul bowed. He had his subject deliver a wooden bow, too. He wound up to the finale.

'When I snap my fingers you will awaken,' he said. 'You will feel completely refreshed as though after a sound sleep. Ten seconds after you awaken you will imagine yourself on a crowded streetcar where no one will give you a seat. You will be extremely tired. Finally, you will ask the fat man opposite you to give you his seat. He will do so and you will sit down. Do you understand?'

Miss Walker nodded her head.

'You will remember nothing of this when you awaken,' Paul said.

He raised his hand to snap his fingers . . .

It was then that Paul Marcus received his mind-jarring idea. He held his hand up, fingers ready to snap, thinking about this idea, until he heard the audience stirring restlessly behind him. Then he shook his head and snapped his fingers.

Miss Walker awakened slowly, looked around, got up, and exactly ten seconds later began the streetcar hallucinations. She performed exactly as commanded, again awakened, and descended confusedly from the stage to more applause and whistles.

It should have been gratifying. But from the moment he received *the* idea, the performance could have involved someone other than Paul Marcus for all of the attention he gave it. Habit carried him through the closing routine, the brief comments on the powers of hypnotism, the curtain calls. Then he walked back to his dressing room slowly, preoccupied, unbuttoning his studs on the way as he always did following the last performance of the night. The concrete cave below stage echoed to his footsteps.

In the dressing room he removed the tailcoat and hung it in the wardrobe. Then he sat down before the dressing table mirror and began to cream his face preparatory to removing the light makeup he wore. He found it hard to meet his own eyes in the mirror.

'This is silly,' he told himself sourly.

A knock sounded at the door. Without turning, he said, 'Come in.'

The door opened hesitantly and the blonde Miss Walker stepped into the room.

'Excuse me,' she said. 'The man at the door said you were in here and . . .'

Seeing her in the mirror, Paul turned around and stood up.

'Is something wrong?' he asked.

Miss Walker looked around her as though to make sure they were alone before she answered.

'Not exactly,' she said.

Paul gestured to a settee beside his dressing table. 'Sit down, won't you?' he asked. He returned to the dressing table as Miss Walker seated herself.

'You'll excuse me if I go on with this chore,' he said, taking a tissue to the grease paint under his chin.

Miss Walker smiled. 'You remind me of a woman at her nightly beauty care,' she said.

Paul thought: Another stage-struck miss, and the performance gives her the excuse to take up my time. He glanced at the girl out of the corners of his eyes. Not bad, though . . .

'You haven't told me to what I owe the pleasure of your company,' he said.

Miss Walker's face clouded with thought.

'It's really very silly,' she said.

Probably, Paul thought.

'Not at all,' he said. 'Tell me what's on your mind.'

'Well, it's an idea I had while my friends were telling me what I did on the stage,' she said. She grinned wryly. 'I had the hardest time believing that there actually wasn't a streetcar up there. I'm still not absolutely convinced. Maybe you brought in a dummy streetcar with a lot of actors. Oh, I don't know!' She shook her head and put a hand to her eyes.

The way she said, 'I don't know!' reminded Paul of his

own idea; *the* idea. He decided to give Miss Walker the fast brush-off in order to devote more time to thinking this new idea through to some logical conclusion.

'What about the streetcar?' he asked.

The girl's face assumed a worried expression. 'I thought I was on a real streetcar,' she said. 'There was no audience, no . . . hypnotist. Nothing. Just the reality of riding the streetcar and being tired like you are after a hard day's work. I saw the people on the car. I smelled them. I felt the car under my feet. I heard the money bounce in the coin-catcher and all the other noises one hears on a streetcar – people talking, a man opening his newspaper. I saw the fat man sitting there in front of me. I asked him for his seat. I even felt embarrassed. I heard him answer and I sat down in his seat. It was warm and I felt the people pressing against me on both sides. It was very real.'

'And what bothers you?' Paul asked.

She looked up from her hands which were tightly clasped in her lap.

'That bothers me,' she said. 'That streetcar. It was real. It was as real as anything I've ever known. It was as real as now. I believed in it. Now I'm told it wasn't real.' Again she looked down at her hands. 'What am I to believe?'

This is getting close to *the* idea, Paul thought.

'Can you express what bothers you in any other way?' he asked.

She looked him squarely in the eyes. 'Yes,' she said. 'I got to thinking while my friends were talking to me. I got to wondering. What if all this –' she gestured around her – 'our whole lives, our world, everything we see, feel, hear, smell, or sense in any way is more of the same. A hypnotic delusion!'

'Precisely!' Paul exhaled the word.

'What did you say?' she asked.

'I said, "Precisely!" '

Her brows drew together. 'Why?'

Paul turned toward her and rested his left elbow on the dressing table. 'Because,' he said, 'at the very moment I was telling you what you would do when you awakened, at the moment I was giving you the commands which resulted in your hallucination, I got the same idea.'

'My goodness!' she said. The very mildness of her exclamation made it seem more vehement than if she had sworn.

Paul turned back to the dressing table mirror. 'I wonder if there could be something in telepathy as well?'

Miss Walker looked at him in the mirror, the room seeming to draw in closely behind her. 'It was an idea I couldn't keep to myself,' she said. 'I told my friends – I came with a married couple – but they just laughed at me. I decided on the spur of the moment to come back here and talk to you and I did it before I could lose my nerve. After all, you're a hypnotist. You should know something about this.'

'It'll take some looking into,' Paul said, 'I wonder . . .' He turned toward Miss Walker. 'Are you engaged tonight?'

Her expression changed. She looked at him as though her mother were whispering in her ear: 'Watch out! Watch out! He's a man.'

'Well, I don't know . . .' she said.

Paul put on his most winning smile. 'I'm no backstage wolf,' he said. 'Please. I feel as though somebody had asked me to cut the Gordian knot, and I'd rather untie it – but I need help.'

'What could we do?' she asked.

It was Paul's turn to hesitate. 'There are several ways to approach the problem,' he said. 'We in America have only scratched the surface in our study of hypnotism.' He doubled up his fist and thudded it gently on the dressing table. 'Hell! I've seen witch doctors in Haiti who know more about it than I do. But . . .'

'What would you do first?' she asked.

'I'd . . . I'd . . .' Paul looked at her for a moment as though he really saw her for the first time. 'I'd do this,' he said. 'Make yourself comfortable on that settee. Lean back. That's it.'

'What are you going to do?' she asked.

'Well,' Paul said, 'it's pretty well established that these sensory hallucinations are centered in one part of the human nervous system which is laid bare by hypnotism. It's possible, by using hypnotism, to get at the commands other hypnotists have put there. I'm going to put you back in deep trance and let you search for the commands yourself. If something is commanding us to live an illusion, the command should be right there with all the others.'

'I don't know,' she said.

'Please,' Paul urged. 'We might be able to crack this thing right here and now in just a few minutes.'

'All right.' She still sounded hesitant, but she leaned back as directed.

Paul lifted his paste gem from the dressing table and focused the table spotlight on it. 'Look at the diamond,' he said. . . .

This time she fell into the trance more readily. Paul checked her for pain threshold, muscular control. She responded appropriately. He began questioning:

'Do you hear my voice?'

'Yes,' she said.

'Do you know what hypnotic commands are in your mind?' he asked.

There was a long pause. Her lips opened dryly. 'There are . . . commands,' she said.

'Do you obey them?' he asked.

'I must.'

'What is the most basic of these commands?' he asked.

'I . . . can . . . not . . . tell.'

Paul almost rubbed his hands. A simple 'Don't talk about it,' he thought.

'Just nod your head if I repeat the command,' he said. 'Does it say, "You must not tell"?'

Her head nodded.

Paul rubbed his hands against his pants legs and realized suddenly that he was perspiring excessively.

'What is it you must not tell?' he asked.

She shook her head without speaking.

'You must tell me,' he said. 'If you do not tell me, your right foot will begin to burn and itch unbearably and will continue to do so until you do tell me. Tell me what it is that you have been commanded not to tell.'

Again she shook her head. She reached down and began to scratch her right foot. She pulled off her shoe.

'You must tell me,' Paul said. 'What is the first word of the command?'

The girl looked up at him, but her eyes remained unfocused.

'You . . .' she said.

It was as though she had brought the word from some dark place deep within her and the saying of it was almost too much to bear. She continued to scratch her right leg.

'What is the second word?' Paul asked.

She tried to speak, but failed.

'Is it "must"?' he asked. 'Nod your head if it is.'

She nodded her head.

'You "must" what?'

Again she was wordless.

He thought about it for a moment. 'Sensory perception,' he thought. He leaned forward. 'Is it "You must sense . . ."?' he asked. 'Is it "You must sense only . . ."?'

She relaxed. Her head nodded and she said, 'Yes.'

Paul took a deep breath.

'What is it "You must sense only . . ."?' he asked.

She opened her mouth, her lips moved, but no sound issued.

He felt like screaming at her, dragging the answer from her mind with his hands.

'What is it?' His voice cracked on the question. 'Tell me!'

She shook her head from side to side. He noticed signs of awakening.

Again he took a deep breath. 'What will happen to you if you tell me?'

'I'll die,' she said.

He leaned forward and lowered his voice to a confidential tone. 'That is foolishness,' he said. 'You can't die just because you say a few words. You know that. Now tell me what it is that you have been ordered to sense.'

She stared straight ahead of her at nothing, mouth open. Paul lowered his head to look directly into her eyes. 'Do you see me?' he asked.

'No,' she said.

'What do you see?' he asked.

'I see death.'

'Look at me instead,' Paul said. 'You remember me.'

'You are death,' she said.

'That's nonsense! Look at me,' he commanded.

Her eyes opened wider. Paul stared into them. Her eyes seemed to grow and grow and grow and grow . . . Paul found himself unable to look away. There was nothing else in the world except two blue-gray eyes. A deep, resonant voice, like a low-register cello, filled his mind.

'You will forget everything that has happened tonight,' it said. 'You will die rather than remember. You will, you *must*, sense only those things which you have been commanded to sense. I, ————————————, command it. Do you remember me?'

Paul's lips formed the word, 'yes'.

'Who am I?' the voice asked.

Paul dampened his dry lips with his tongue. 'You are death,' he said.

Bureaucracy has a kind of timeless, raceless mold which makes its communiques recognizable as to type by the members of any bureau anywhere. The multiple copies, the precise wording to cover devious intent, the absolute protocol of address – all are of a pattern, whether the communication is to the Reconstruction Finance Corporation or the Denebian Bureau of Indoctrination.

Mirsar Wees knew the pattern as another instinct. He had been supervisor of indoctrination and overseer of the korad farming on Sol III for one hundred and fifty-seven of the planet's years. In that time, by faithfully following the letter of the Indoctrination Bureau's code and never an individual interpretation of its spirit, he had insured for himself a promotion to Coordinator of the entire Sol prefecture whenever such an opening occurred.

Having met another threat to his position and resolved it, knowing the security of his tenure, he sat before the mechanical secretary-transmitter in his office and dictated a letter to the Bureau. The vision-ring around his head glowed a dull amber as he relaxed the receptors in it. His body stretched out comfortably, taking a gentle massage from the chair.

'There has been considerable carelessness lately with the training of neo-indoctrinators,' he said into the communo-tube.

Let a few heads fall at the bureau, he thought.

'There seems to be a feeling that, because we of the Sol prefecture are dealing with lesser beings, a lesser amount of care need be taken with the prefecture's indoctrinators. I have just dealt with a first-order threat to the Sol III korad supply, a threat which was directly attributable to neo-indoctrinator carelessness. A deviant was allowed to pass through the hands of three of our latest acquisitions from the College of Indoctrinators. These indoctrinators have been sent back for retraining.'

He thought in satisfaction: They will reflect that the korad secreted by the glands of our charges is necessary for their own immortality, and will be more severe at the training center because of that. And pensively: It is almost time for me to tell them of our breeding experiments to bring the korad glands to the exterior of these creatures, making more frequent draining possible. They will particularly appreciate the niceties of indoctrination – increasing the mating pattern, increasing individual peril and, thereby, the longevity gland secretion, and the more strict visual limitation to keep the creatures from discovering the change. . . .

'I am sending a complete visio-corder report on how I

met this threat,' he spoke into the tube. 'Briefly, I insinuated myself into the earth-being's presence and installed a more severe command. Standard procedure. It was not deemed practical to eliminate the creature because of the latest interpretations on command interference; it was felt that the being's elimination might set off further thought-patterns inimical to our designs.

'The creature was, therefore, commanded to mate with another of its ilk who is more stringently under our control. The creature also was removed from any labor involving the higher nerve-centers and has been put to another task, that of operating a transportation device called a streetcar.

'The mate has been subjected to the amputation of an appendage. Unfortunately, before I could take action, the creature I treated had started along an exceedingly clever line of action and had installed irremovable commands which made the appendage useless.'

They will see how much of a deviant the creature was, he thought, and how careless the new indoctrinators were.

'The indoctrinator service must keep in mind at all times what happened to create the Sol planetoid belt. Those bodies, as we all know, once were the planet Dirad, the greatest korad source in the entire galaxy. Slipshod procedure employed by indoctrinators set up a situation similar to the one I have just nipped, and we were forced to destroy the entire planet. The potency of minds which have slipped from our control should be kept constantly before our attention. Dirad is an object lesson.

'The situation here is again completely normal, of course, and the korad supply is safe. We can go on draining the immortality of others – but *only as long as we maintain constant vigilance.*'

He signed it, 'Cordially, Mirsar Wees, Chief Indoctrinator, Sol Sub-prefecture.'

Someday, he thought, it will be 'Coordinator.'

Rising from the mechano-secretary, Mirsar Wees moved over to the 'incoming' tube of his report-panel and noticed a tube which his new assistant had tabbed with the yellow band of 'extreme importance.'

He inserted the tube into a translator, sat down, and watched as it dealt out the report:

'A Hindu creature has seen itself as it really is,' the report said.

Mirsar Wees reached over and put a tracer-beam on his new assistant to observe how that worthy was meeting this threat.

The report buzzed on: 'The creature went insane as per indoctrination command, but most unfortunately it is a member of a sect which worships insanity. Others are beginning to listen to its babblings.'

The report concluded: 'I make haste.'

Mirsar Wees leaned back, relaxed and smiled blandly. The new assistant showed promise.

THE GONE DOGS

A green turbo-copter moved over the New Mexico sand flats, its rotor blades going whik-whik-whik. Evening sunlight cast deep shadows ahead of it where the ground shelved away to a river canyon. The 'copter settled to a rock outcropping, a hatch popped open and a steel cage containing one female coyote was thrown out. The cage door fell away. In one jump, the animal was out of its prison and running. It whisked over the outcropping, leaped down to a ledge along the canyon wall and was out of sight around a bend – in its blood a mutated virus which had started with hog cholera.

The lab had a sharp chemical odor in which could be detected iodoform and ether. Under it was that musky, wet-fur smell found in the presence of caged animals. A despondent fox terrier sulked in a cage at one end; the remains of a poodle were stretched on a dissecting board atop a central bench, a tag on its leg labeled *X-8 PULLMAN VETERINARY RESEARCH CENTER, LABORATORY E*. Indirect lighting touched everything with a shadowless indifference.

Biologist Varley Trent, a lanky, dark-haired man with angular features, put his scalpel in a tray beside the poodle, stepped back, looked across at Dr Walter Han-Meers, professor of veterinary medicine. The professor was a plump, sandy-haired Chinese-Dutchman with the smooth-skinned looked of an Oriental idol. He stood beside the dissecting bench, staring at the poodle.

'Another failure,' said Trent. 'Each one of these I autopsy, I say to myself we're that much closer to the last dog on Earth.'

The professor nodded. 'Came down to give you the

latest. Don't see how it helps us, but for what it's worth, this virus started in coyote.'

'Coyote?'

Professor Han-Meers found a lab stool, pulled it up, sat down. 'Yes. Ranch hand in New Mexico broke it. Talked to the authorities. His boss, a fellow named Porter Durkin, is a VMD, has a veterinary hospital on a ranch down there. Hoped to make a name for himself, killing off all the coyotes. Made a name for himself all right. Government had to move in troops to keep him from being lynched.'

Trent ran a hand through his hair. 'Didn't the fool realize his disease would spread to other canines?'

'Apparently didn't even think of it. He has a license from one of those little hogwallow colleges, but I don't see how anyone that stupid could make the grade.'

'How about the coyote?'

'Oh, that was a great success. Sheep ranchers say they haven't lost an animal to coyotes in over a month. Only things worrying them now are bears, cougars and the lack of dogs to . . .'

'Speaking of dogs,' said Trent, 'we're going to need more test animals here by tomorrow. Serum nine isn't doing a thing for that fox terrier. He'll die tonight sometime.'

'We'll have lots of test animals by tomorrow,' said Han-Meers. 'The last two dog isolation preserves in Canada reported primary infestations this morning.'

Trent drummed his fingers on the bench top. 'What's the government doing about the offer from the Vegan biophysicists?'

Han-Meers shrugged. 'We are still turning them down. The Vegans are holding out for full control of the project. You know their reputation for bio-physical alterations. They might be able to save our dogs for us, but what we'd get back wouldn't be a dog any longer. It'd be some elongated, multi-legged, scaly-tailed monstrosity. I wish I knew why they went in for those fish-tail types.'

'Linked gene,' said Trent. 'Intelligence factor coupled.

They use their *mikeses* generators to open up the gene pairs and . . .'

'That's right,' said Han-Meers. 'You studied with them. What's the name of that Vegan you're always talking about?'

'Ger (whistle) Anso-Anso.'

'That's the one. Isn't he on Earth with the Vegan delegation?'

Trent nodded. 'I met him at the Quebec conference ten years ago – the year before we made the bio-physical survey to Vega. He's really a nice fellow once you get to know him.'

'Not for me.' Han-Meers shook his head. 'They're too tall and disdainful. Makes me feel inferior. Always harping about their damned *mikeses* generators and what they can do in bio-physics.'

'They can do it, too.'

'That's what makes them so damned irritating!'

Trent laughed. 'If it'll make you feel any better, the Vegans may be all puffed up with pride about their bio-physics, but they're jealous as all git-out over our tool facility.'

'Hmmmph!' said Han-Meers.

'I still think we should send them dogs for experimental purposes,' said Trent. 'The Lord knows we're not going to have any dogs left pretty soon at the rate we're going.'

'We won't send them a sick spaniel as long as Gilberto Nathal is in the Federated Senate,' said Han-Meers. 'Every time the subject comes up, he jumps to his feet and hollers about the pride of Earth and the out-worlder threat.'

'But . . .'

'It hasn't been too long since the Denebian campaign,' said Han-Meers.

Trent wet his lips with his tongue. 'Mmmmm, hmmmm. How are the other research centers coming?'

'Same as we are. The morning report shows a lot of words which sum up to a big round zero.' Han-Meers reached into his pocket, extracted a yellow sheet of paper.

'Here, you may as well see this. It'll be out pretty soon, anyway.' He thrust the paper into Trent's hand.

Trent glanced at the heading:

BUREAU-GRAM – DEPARTMENT OF HEALTH AND SANITATION – PRIMARY SECRET:

He looked up at Han-Meers.

'Read it,' said the professor.

Trent looked back to the *bureau-gram*. 'Department doctors today confirmed that Virus D-D which is attacking the world's canines is one-hundred percent fatal. In spite of all quarantine precautions it is spreading. The virus shows kinship to hog cholera, but will thrive in a solution of protomycetin strong enough to kill any other virus on the list. It shows ability to become dormant and anerobic. Unless a suitable weapon with which to combat this disease is found within two more months, Earth is in danger of losing its entire population of wolves, dogs, foxes, coyote . . .'

Trent looked back to Han-Meers. 'We've all suspected it was this bad, but . . .' He tapped the *bureau-gram*.

Han-Meers slipped the paper from Trent's grasp. 'Varley, you held out on the census takers when they came around counting dogs, didn't you?'

Trent pursed his lips. 'What makes you say a thing like that?'

'Varley, I wouldn't turn you over to the police. I am suggesting you contact your Vegan and give him your dogs.'

Trent took a deep breath. 'I gave him five puppies last week.'

A Capital correspondent for a news service had broken the story six weeks previously, following up a leak in the Health and Sanitation Committee of the Federated Senate. A new virus was attacking the world's canine population and no means of fighting it was known. People already realized their pets were dying off in droves. The news story was enough to cause a panic. Interstellar passenger space

disappeared. Powerful men exerted influence for themselves and friends. People ran every which way with their
pets, hopelessly tangling inter-world quarantine restrictions.
And the inevitable rackets appeared.

*SPECIAL CHARTER SHIP TO PLANETS OF AL-
DEBARAN. STRICTEST QUARANTINE REQUIRE-
MENTS. TRAINED ATTENDANTS TO GUARD
YOUR PETS IN TRANSIT. PRICE: FIFTY THOU-
SAND CREDITS A KILO.*

The owners, of course, could not accompany their pets,
shipping space being limited.

This racket was stopped when a Federation patrol ship
ran into a strange meteor swarm beyond Pluto, stopped
to map its course, discovered the swarm was composed of
the frozen bodies of dogs.

Eleven days after the virus story appeared, the Arcturian
planets banned Terran dogs. The Arcturians knew dog-
smuggling would begin and their people could profit.

Trent kept six part-beagle hounds in a servo-mech kennel
at an Olympic Mountain hunting camp. They were at the
camp when the government instituted its emergency census
of dogs. Trent deliberately overlooked mentioning them.

Leaving Pullman at three o'clock the morning after he
talked to Han-Meers, he put his jet-'copter on auto-pilot,
slept until he reached Aberdeen.

The Aberdeen commander of the Federated Police was
a graying, burn-scarred veteran of the Denebian campaign.
His office was a square room overlooking the harbor. The
walls were hung with out-world weapons, group photo-
graphs of officers and men. The commander stood up as
Trent entered, waved him to a chair. 'Makaroff's the name.
What can I do for you?'

Trent introduced himself, sat down, explained that he
was a member of the Pullman research staff, that he had
nine hounds – six adults and three puppies – at a mountain
kennel.

The commander seated himself, grasped the arms of his

chair, leaned back. 'Why aren't they in one of the government preserves?'

Trent looked the man in the eyes. 'Because I was convinced they'd be safer where they are and I was right. The preserves are infested. Yet my hounds are in perfect health. What's more, Commander, I've discovered that humans are carrying the disease. We . . .'

'You mean if I pet a dog that could kill it?'

'That's right.'

The commander fell silent. Presently, he said, 'So you disobeyed the quarantine act, eh?'

'Yes.'

'I've done the same kind of thing myself on occasion,' said the commander. 'You see some stupid order given, you know it won't work; so you go against it. If you're wrong they throw the book at you; if you're right they pin a medal on you. I remember one time in the Denebian campaign when . . .'

'Could you put an air patrol over my camp?' asked Trent.

The commander pulled at his chin. 'Hounds eh? Nothing better than a good hunting hound. Damned shame to see them die with all the rest.' He paused. 'Air patrol, eh? No humans?'

'We have two months to find an answer to this virus or there won't be another dog on earth,' said Trent. 'You see how important those dogs could be?'

'Bad as that, eh?' He pulled a vidi-phone to him. 'Get me Perlan.' He turned to Trent. 'Where is your camp?'

Trent gave him the vectors. The commander scribbled them on a scratch pad.

A face came on the screen. 'Yes, sir.'

The commander turned back to the vidi-phone. 'Perlan, I want a robotics air patrol – twenty-four-hour duty – over a hunting camp at,' he glanced at the scratch pad, 'vectors 8181-A and 0662-Y, Olympic West Slope. There's a kennel at the camp with nine hounds in it. No humans at all must contact those dogs.' He wet his lips with his tongue. 'A doctor has just told me that humans are carrying this Virus D-D thing.'

When Trent landed at Pullman that afternoon he found Han-Meers waiting in Lab E. The professor sat on the same stool as though he had not moved in two days. His slant eyes contemplated the cage which had held the fox terrier. Now there was an airedale in the enclosure. As Trent entered, Han-Meers turned.

'Varley, what is this the Aberdeen policeman tells the news services?'

Trent closed the lab door. *So the Commander had talked.*

'Flores Clinic was on the line twice today,' said Han-Meers. 'Want to know what we discovered that they overlooked. The policeman has perhaps made up a story?'

Trent shook his head. 'No. I told him a hunch of mine was an actual fact. I had to get an air patrol over my hunting camp. Those hounds are in perfect health.'

Han-Meers nodded. 'They have been without such a convenience all summer. Now they have to have it.'

'I've been afraid they were dead. After all, I raised those hounds from pups. We've hunted and ...'

'I see. And tomorrow we tell everybody it was a big mistake. I had thought you possessed more scientific integrity than that.'

Trent hid his anger behind a passive face, slipped off his coat, donned a lab smock. 'My dogs were isolated from humans all summer. We ...'

'The Flores people have been thorough in their investigation,' said Han-Meers. 'They suspect we are trying to ...'

'Not thorough enough.' Trent opened a cupboard door, took out a bottle of green liquid. 'Are you going to stay here and help or are you going to let me tackle this one alone?'

Han-Meers took off his coat, found an extra lab smock. 'You are out on a thin limb, Varley.' He turned, smiled.

'But what a wonderful opportunity to give those MDs a really big come-uppance.'

At nine-sixteen the next morning, Trent dropped a glass beaker. It shattered on the tile floor and Trent's calm shattered with it. He cursed for two minutes.

'We are tired,' said Han-Meers. 'We will rest, come back to it later. I will put off the Flores people and the others today. There is still . . .'

'No.' Trent shook his head. 'We're going to take another skin wash on me with Clarendon's Astringent.'

'But we've already tried that twice and . . .'

'Once more,' said Trent. 'This time we'll add the synthetic dog blood *before* fractionating.'

At ten-twenty-two, Han-Meers set the final test tube in a plastic diffraction rack, pressed a switch at its base. A small silver cobweb shimmered near the top of the tube.

'Ahhhhhh!' said the professor.

They traced back. By noon they had the pattern: Dormant virus was carried in the human glands of perspiration, coming out through the pores – mostly in the palms of the hands – only under stress of emotion. Once out of the pores, the virus dried, became anerobic.

'If I hadn't dropped that beaker and become angry,' said Trent.

'We would still be looking,' added Han-Meers. 'Devil of a one, this. Dormant and in minute quantity. That is why they missed it. Who tests an excited subject? They wait for him to become calm.'

'Each man kills the thing he loves,' quoted Trent.

'Should pay more attention to philosophers like Oscar Wilde,' said Han-Meers. 'Now I will call the doctors, tell them of their error. They are not going to like a mere biologist showing them up.'

'It was an accident,' said Trent.

'An accident based on observation of your dogs,' said Han-Meers. 'It is, of course, not the first time such accidents have occurred to mere biologists. There was Pasteur. They had him stoned in the village streets for . . . '

'Pasteur was a chemist,' said Trent curtly. He turned, put test tube and stand on a side bench. 'We'll have to tell the authorities to set up robotics service for the remaining dogs. That may give us time to see this thing through.'

'I will use your lab phone to call the doctors,' said Han-Meers. 'I cannot wait to hear that Flores' voice when . . .'

The phone rang. Han-Meers put it to his ear. 'Yes. I am me . . . I mean, I am here. Yes, I will take the call.' He waited. 'Oh, hello, Dr Flores. I was just about to . . .' Han-Meers fell silent, listened. 'Oh, you did?' His voice was flat. 'Yes, that agrees with our findings. Yes, through the pores of the hands mostly. We were waiting to confirm it, to be certain . . . Yes, by our Dr Trent. He's a biologist on the staff here. I believe some of your people were his students. Brilliant fellow. Deserves full credit for the discovery.' There was a long silence. 'I insist on scientific integrity, Dr Flores, and I have your report in my hands. It absolves humans as carriers of the virus. I agree that this development will be bad for your clinic, but that cannot be helped. Good-bye, Dr Flores. Thank you for calling.' He hung up the phone, turned. Trent was nowhere in sight.

That afternoon the last remaining pureblood Saint Bernard died at Angúac, Manitoba. By the following morning, Georgian officials had confirmed that their isolation kennels near Igurtsk were infested. The search for uninfected dogs continued, conducted now by robots. In all the world there were nine dogs known to be free of Virus D-D – six adult hounds and three puppies. They sniffed around their mountain kennel, despondent at the lack of human companionship.

When Trent arrived at his bachelor apartment that night he found a visitor, a tall (almost seven feet) Class C humanoid, head topped by twin, feather-haired crests, eyes shaded by slitted membranes like Venetian blinds. His slender body was covered by a blue robe, belted at the waist.

'Ger!' said Trent. He shut the door.

'Friend Varley,' said the Vegan in his odd, whistling tones.

They held out their hands, pressed palms together in the Vegan fashion. Ger's seven-fingered hands felt over-warm.

'You've a fever,' said Trent. 'You've been too long on Earth.'

'It is the accursed oxidized iron in your environment,' said Ger. 'I will take an increased dosage of medicine to-night.' He relaxed his crests, a gesture denoting pleasure. 'But it is good to see you again, Varley.'

'And you,' said Trent. 'How are the . . .' He put a hand down, made the motion of petting a dog.

'That is why I came,' said Ger. 'We need more.'

'More? Are the others dead?'

'Their cells are alive in new descendants,' said Ger. 'We used an acceleration chamber to get several generations quickly, but we are not satisfied with the results. Those were very strange animals, Varley. Is it not peculiar that they were identical in appearance?'

'It sometimes happens,' said Trent.

'And the number of chromosomes,' said Ger. 'Aren't there . . .'

'Some special breeds differ,' said Trent hurriedly.

'Oh.' Ger nodded his head. 'Do you have more of this breed we may take?'

'It'll be tricky to do,' said Trent, 'but maybe if we are very careful, we can get away with it.'

Commander Makaroff was *delighted* to renew his acquaintance with the famous Dr Trent. He was *delighted* to meet the visitor from far Vega, although a little less delighted. It was clear the commander was generally suspicious of out-worlders. He ushered the two into his office, seated them, took his place behind his desk.

'I'd like a pass permitting Dr Anso-Anso to visit my

kennel,' said Trent. 'Not being an Earth-human, he does not carry the virus and it will be quite safe to . . .'

'Why?'

'You have, perhaps, heard of the Vegan skill in bio-physics,' said Trent. 'Dr Anso-Anso is assisting me in a line of research. He needs to take several blood and culture samples from . . .'

'Couldn't a robot do it?'

'The observations depend on highly specialized knowl-edge and there are no robots with this training.'

'Hmmm.' Commander Makaroff considered this. 'I see. Well, if you vouch for him, Dr Trent, I'm sure he's all right.' His tone suggested that Dr Trent *could be* mistaken. He took a pad from a drawer, scrawled a pass, handed it to Trent. 'I'll have a police 'copter take you in.'

'We have a specially sterilized 'copter with our lab equipment,' said Trent. 'Robotics International is servic-ing it right now.'

Commander Makaroff nodded. 'I see. Then I'll have an escort ready for you whenever you say.'

The summons came the next day on a pink sheet of paper:

'Dr Varley Trent is ordered to appear tomorrow before the special sub-committee of the Federated Senate Com-mittee on Health and Sanitation at a hearing to be con-ducted at 4pm in the office building of the Federated Senate.' It was signed, 'Oscar Olaffson, special assistant to Sen. Gilberto Nathal.'

Trent accepted the summons in his lab, read it, took it up to Han-Meers' office.

The professor read the order, handed it back to Trent. 'Nothing is said about charges, Varley. Where were you yesterday?'

Trent sat down. 'I got my Vegan friend into the preserve so he could snatch the three puppies. He's half way home with them by this time.'

'They discovered it on the morning count, of course,' said Han-Meers. 'Ordinarily, they'd have just hauled you off to jail, but there's an election coming up. Nathal must be cozy with your Commander Makaroff.'

Trent looked at the floor.

'The Senator will crucify you in spite of your virus discovery,' said Han-Meers. 'I'm afraid you've made powerful enemies. Dr Flores is the brother-in-law of Senator Grapopulus of the Appropriations Committee. They'll bring in Flores Clinic people to claim that the virus carrier could have been discovered without you.'

'But they're my dogs! I can . . .'

'Not since the emergency census and quarantine act,' said Han-Meers. 'You're guilty of sequestering government property.' He pointed a finger at Trent. 'And these enemies you've made will . . .'

'I've made! You were the one had to pull the grandstand act with Flores.'

'Now, Varley. Let's not quarrel among ourselves.'

Trent looked at the floor. 'Okay. What's done is done.'

'I have a little idea,' said Han-Meers. 'The college survey ship, the Elmendorff, is out at Hartley Field. It has been fueled and fitted for a trip to Sagittarius.'

'What does that mean?'

'The ship is well guarded, of course, but a known member of the staff with a forged note from me could get aboard. Could you handle the Elmendorff alone?'

'Certainly. That's the ship we took to Vega on the biophysical survey.'

'Then run for it. Get that ship into hyper-drive and they'll never catch you.'

Trent shook his head. 'That would be admitting my guilt.'

'Man, you are guilty! Senator Nathal is going to discover that tomorrow. It'll be big news. But if you run away, that will be bigger news and the senator's screaming will be just so much more background noise.'

'I don't know.'

'People are tired of his noises, Varley.'

'I still don't like it.'

'Varley, the senator is desperate for vote-getting news. Give him a little more time, a little more desperation, he'll go too far.'

'I'm not worried about the senator. I'm worried about . . .'

'The dogs,' said Han-Meers. 'And if you escaped to Vega you could give them the benefit of your knowledge of terrestrial biology. You'd have to do it by remote control, of course, but . . .' He left the idea dangling there.

Trent pursed his lips.

'Every minute you waste makes your chances of escape that much slimmer.' Han-Meers pushed a pad toward Trent. 'Here's my letterhead. Forge your note.'

Twenty minutes after Trent's 'copter took off for Hartley Field, a government 'copter settled to the campus parking area. Two men emerged, hurried to Han-Meers' office, presented police credentials. 'We're looking for a Dr Varley Trent. He's charged with violating the dog-restriction act. He's to be held in custody.'

Han-Meers looked properly horrified. 'I think he went home. He said something about not feeling well.'

Senator Nathal raged. His plump body quivered. His normally red face became redder. He shouted, he screamed. His fuming countenance could be seen nightly on video. Just when he was reaching a fine climax, warning people against unbridled science, he was pushed aside by more important news.

The last dog in an isolation preserve – a brindle chow – died from virus infection. Before the senator could build up steam for a new attack, the government announced the discovery of an Arctic wolf pack of twenty-six animals untouched by virus. A day later, robot searchers turned up a live twelve-year-old mongrel on Easter Island and five cocker spaniels on Tierra del Fuego. Separate preserves for dogs and wolves were prepared on the west slope of the Olympic Mountains, all of the animals transported there.

Wolves, cockers, mongrel and hounds – they were the

world's pets. Excursions in sealed 'copters were operated from Aberdeen to a point five kilometers from the dog-wolf preserve. There, powerful glasses sometimes gave a glimpse of motion which imagination could pad into a dog or wolf.

About the time Senator Nathal was getting ready to launch a new blast, pointing out that Trent's hounds were not necessarily important, that there had been other canine survivors, the twelve-year-old mongrel died of old age.

Dog lovers of the world mourned. The press took over and all the glory of mongreldom was rehashed. Senator Nathal again was background noise.

Trent headed for Vega, hit hyper-drive as soon as he had cleared the sun's area of warp. He knew that the Vegans would have to quarantine him to protect the dogs, but he could follow the experiments on video, help with his knowledge of terrestrial biology.

Professor Han-Meers, protesting ill health, turned his college duties over to an assistant, went on a vacation tour of the world. First, he stopped at the capital, met Senator Nathal, apologized for Dr Trent's defection and praised the politician's stand.

In Geneva, Han-Meers met a pianist whose pet Dalmatians had been among the first to die in the epidemic. At Cairo, he met a government official who had bred wolf hounds, also among the first deceased. In Paris, he met the wife of a furrier whose pet airedale, *Coco*, had died in the third wave of the epidemic. In Moscow, in Bombay, in Calcutta, in Singapore, in Peking, in San Francisco, in Des Moines, in Chicago, he met others in like circumstances. To all he gave notes of introduction to Senator Nathal, explaining that the senator would see they received special treatment if they wanted to visit the Olympic preserve. Han-Meers expected at least one of these people to become a scandalous nuisance sufficient to ensure the senator's political embarrassment.

The wife of the Paris furrier, Mme Estagién Couloc, paid off, but in a manner Han-Meers had not anticipated.

Mme Couloc was a slim woman of perhaps forty-five, chic in the timeless French fashion, childless, with a narrow, haughty face and a manner to match it. But her grandmother had been a farm wife and underneath the surface of pampered rich woman, Mme Couloc was tough. She came to Aberdeen complete with two maids, a small Alp of luggage and a note from Senator Nathal. She had convinced herself that all of this *nonsense* about humans carrying the disease couldn't possibly apply to her. *A few simple sanitary precautions and she could have a dog of her own.*

Mme Couloc meant to have a part-beagle dog, no matter the cost. The fact that there were no dogs to be had, made her need all the more urgent. Cautious inquiries at Aberdeen convinced her this would have to be a lone-handed job. Amidst the tangled psychological desperation which filled her mind, she worked out a plan which had all of the evasive cunning characteristic of the mentally ill.

From the air, on one of the daily excursions, Mme Couloc surveyed the terrain. It was rugged enough to discourage a less determined person. The area had been maintained in its natural state for seven hundred years. Thick undergrowth of salal, devil club and huckleberry crowded the natural avenues of access to the interior. Rivers were full of the spring snow melt. Ridgetops were tangles of windfalls, wild blackberries in the burns, granite outcroppings. After the rough terrain there was a double fence – each unit sixteen meters high, a kilometer between.

Mme Couloc returned to Aberdeen, left her maids at the hotel, flew to Seattle where she bought tough camping clothes, a rope and grappling hook, a light pack, concentrated food and a compass. A map of the preserve was easy to obtain. They were sold as souvenirs.

Then she went fishing in the Straits of Juan de Fuca,

staying at Neah Bay. To the south towered the Olympics, remote snow caps.

For three days it rained; five days Mme Couloc fished with a guide. On the ninth day she went fishing alone. The next morning, the Federated Coast Guard picked up her overturned boat off Tatoosh Light. By that time she was nineteen kilometers south of Sequim, two kilometers inside the prohibited area which surrounded the fences. She slept all day in a spruce thicket. Moonlight helped her that night, but it took the entire night for her to come within sight of the fence. That day she crouched in a tangle of Oregon grape bushes, saw two tripod-legged robot patrols pass on the other side of the fence. At nightfall she moved forward, waited for a patrol to pass and go out of sight. The grapple and rope took her over the top. The kilometer between fences was cleared of trees and underbrush. She crossed it swiftly, scaled the final barrier.

The robotics patrol had counted too heavily on the forbidding terrain and they had not figured a psychotic woman into their plans.

Two kilometers inside the preserve. Mme Couloc found a cedar copse in which to hide. Her heart racing, she crouched in the copse, waiting for the dawn in which to find *her dog*. There were scratches on her face, hands and legs; her clothes were torn. *But she was inside!*

Several times that night she had to dry her perspiring palms against her khaki hiking trousers. Toward morning, she fell asleep on the cold ground. Bess and Eagle found her there just after dawn.

Mme Couloc awoke to the scraping of a warm, damp tongue against her cheek. For a moment, she thought it was her dead *Coco*. Then she realized where she was.

And the beautiful dogs!

She threw her arms around Bess, who was as starved for human affection as was Mme Couloc.

Oh, you beautifuls!

The robotics patrol found them there shortly before noon. The robots were counting dogs with the aid of the tiny transmitters they had imbedded in the flesh of each animal. Mme Couloc had been waiting for nightfall in which to escape with a dog.

Bess and Eagle ran from the robots. Mme Couloc screamed and raged as the impersonal mechanicals took her away.

That afternoon, Eagle touched noses with a wolf female through the fence separating their enclosures.

Although the robots put each dog in isolation, they were too late. And nobody thought to bother with the wolves in their separate preserve.

In seven weeks the dog-wolf preserves were emptied by Virus D-D. Mme Couloc was sent to a mental hospital in spite of the pleas of an expensive lawyer. The news services made much of Senator Nathal's note which had been found in her pocket.

Earth officials sent a contrite message to Vega. It was understood, said the message, that one Dr Varley Trent had given Earth dogs to a Vegan bio-physicist. Were there, by any chance, some dogs still alive?

Back came the Vegan reply: *We have no dogs. We do not know the present whereabouts of Dr Trent.*

Trent's ship came out of hyper-drive with Vega large in the screens. The sun's flaming prominences were clearly visible. At eight hundred thousand kilometers, he increased magnification, began scanning for the planet. Instead, he picked up a Vegan guard ship arrowing toward him. The Vegan was only six thousand kilometers off when it launched a torpedo. The proximity explosion cut off Trent's quick leap for the transmitter to give his identity. The ship buckled and rocked. Emergency doors slammed, air hissed, warning lights came on, bells clanged. Trent scrambled to the only lifeboat remaining in his section. The tiny escape craft was still serviceable, although its transmitter was cracked open.

He kept the lifeboat in the shadow of his ship's wreckage

as long as he could, then dove for the Vegan planet which
loomed at two o'clock on his screen. As soon as his driver
tubes came alight, the Vegan sped after him. Trent pushed
the little boat to its limit, but the pursuer still gained. They
were too close to the planet now for the Vegan to use
another torpedo.

The lifeboat screamed into the thin edge of the atmosphere. *Too fast!* The air-cooling unit howled with the overload. A rear surface control flared red, melted, fused. Trent
had time to fire the emergency nose rockets, cut in automatic pilot before he blacked out. The ship dived, partly
out of control, nose rockets still firing. Relays clicked –
full alarm! – circuits designed to guard human life in an
emergency came alive. Some worked, some had been
destroyed.

Somewhere, he could hear running water. It was dark
where he was, or perhaps lighted by a faint redness. His
eyelids were stuck tightly. He could feel folds of cloth
around him. A parachute! The robot controls of the lifeboat had ejected him in the chute-seat as a last resort.

Trent tried to move. His muscles refused to obey. He
could sense numbness in his hips, a tingling loss of specific
perception in his arms.

Then he heard it – the baying of a hound – far and
clear. It was a sound he had never again expected to hear.
The bugling note was repeated. It reminded him of frosty
nights on Earth, following Bess and Eagle and . . .

The baying of a hound!

Panic swept through him. The hound mustn't find him!
He was Earth-human, loaded with deadly virus!

Straining at his cheek muscle, Trent managed to open
one eye, saw that it was not dark, but a kind of yellow
twilight under the folds of the parachute. His eyelids had
been clotted with blood.

Now he could hear running feet, a hound's eager sniff-
ing.

Please keep him away from me! he begged.

An edge of the chute stirred. Now there was an eager whining. Something crept toward him under the cloth.

'Go away!' he croaked.

Through the blurred vision of his one eye, Trent saw a brown and white head – very like Eagle's. It bent toward something. With a sick feeling, Trent realized that the *something* was one of his own outstretched, virus-filled hands. He saw a pink tongue come out, lick the hand, but could not feel it. He tried to move and unconsciousness overwhelmed him. One last thought flitted through his mind before the darkness came—

'*Each man kills the thing he . . .*'

There was a bed beneath him – soft, sleep-lulling. In one part of his mind he knew a long time had passed. There had been hands, needles, wheeled carts taking him places, liquids in his mouth, tubes in his veins. He opened his eyes. Green walls, glaring white sunshine partially diffused by louvre shutters, a glimpse of blue-green hills outside.

'You are feeling better?' The voice had the peculiar whistling aspiration of the Vegan vocals.

Trent shifted his gaze to the right. Ger! The Vegan stood beside the bed, deceptively Earth-human in appearance. His shutter-like eye membranes were opened wide, the double crest of feathery hair retracted. He wore a yellow robe belted at the waist.

'How long . . .'

The Vegan put a seven-fingered hand on Trent's wrist, felt the pulse. 'Yes, you are feeling much better. You have been very ill for almost four of your months.'

'Then the dogs are all dead,' said Trent, his voice flat.

'Dead?' Ger's eye membranes flicked closed, opened.

'I killed them,' said Trent. 'My body's loaded with dormant virus.'

'No,' said the Vegan. 'We gave the dogs an extra white blood cell – more predatory. Your puny virus could not survive it.'

Trent tried to sit up, but Ger restrained him. 'Please, Varley. You are not yet recovered.'

'But if the dogs are immune to the virus . . .' He shook his head. 'Give me a shipload of dogs and you can name your own price.'

'Varley, I did not say dogs are immune. They . . . are . . . not like dogs exactly. We cannot give you a shipload of your animals because we do not have them. They were sacrificed in our work.'

Trent stared at him.

'I have unfortunate news, my friend. We have made our planet restricted to humans. You may live out your life here, but you may not communicate with your fellows.'

'Is that why your ship fired on me?'

'We thought it was an Earth vessel coming to investigate.'

'But . . .'

'It is regrettable that yourself must be kept here, Varley, but the pride of our peoples is at stake.'

'Pride?'

The Vegan looked at the floor. 'We, who have never failed a bio-physical alteration . . .' He shook his head.

'What happened?'

The Vegan's face went blue with embarrassment.

Trent recalled his first awakening on this planet. 'When I recovered consciousness I saw a dog. At least I saw its head.'

Ger pulled a wicker chair close to the bed, sat down. 'Varley, we tried to combine the best elements of our own *progoas* and the Earth dogs.'

'Well, wasn't that what you were supposed to do?'

'Yes, but in the process we lost all of the dogs you sent us and the resultant animals . . .' He shrugged.

'What are they?'

'They do not have a scaly tail or horned snout. For centuries we have been telling the Universe that sentient pets of the highest quality must show these characteristics of our own *progoas*.'

'Aren't the new animals intelligent and loyal? Do they have as good hearing, sense of smell?'

'If anything, these characteristics have been heightened.' He paused. 'You realize, though, that this animal is not truly a dog.'

'Not truly a . . .'

'It's fully serviceable . . .'

Trent swallowed. 'Then you can name your own price.'

'When we made our first cross, the *mikeses* fertilization process united an open *progoa* cell with a dog cell, but a series of peculiar linkages occurred. They were not what we had come to expect from our readings and from what you had told us.'

Trent took a deep breath, exhaled slowly.

'It was as though the gene pattern of dog characteristics were predatory, tying down tightly even with *progoa* dominants,' said Ger. 'Each time we repeated the process, the same thing occurred. From our knowledge of terrestrial biology, this should not have been. The blood chemistry of our animals is based on the element you call copper. We have not much iron on our planet, but what few of your type of animals we had proved to us that the copper-basic was dominant in a *mikeses* cross. Of course, without a *mikeses* generator, cells cannot be opened to permit such a cross, but still . . .'

Trent closed his eyes, opened them. 'No one else will ever hear what I am about to tell you . . .' He hesitated.

Vertical lines of thoughtfulness appeared in the Vegan's cheeks. 'Yes?'

'When I was here on the survey trip, I copied the diagram of a *mikeses* generator. I was able to build a working model on Earth. With it, I developed a line of hounds.' He wet his lips with his tongue. 'We have life on Earth with blood of copper-base chemistry. The common squid of our oceans is one of them.'

Ger lowered his chin, continued to stare at Trent.

'With the generator, I linked the canine dominants of my dogs with a recessive of squid.'

'But they could not breed naturally. They . . .'

'Of course not. The hounds I sent you were from a line which had no fathers for six generations. I fertilized them with the generator. They had only the female side, open to the first linkage which presented itself.'

'Why?'

'Because, from my observations of *progoas*, I knew dogs were superior, but could profit by such a cross. I hoped to make that cross myself.'

The Vegan looked at the floor. 'Varley, it pains me, but I am faced with the evidence that your claim is true. However, the pride of my world would never permit this to be known. Perhaps the Elders should reconsider.'

'You know me,' said Trent. 'You have my word on it.'

Ger nodded. 'It is as you say, Varley. I know you.' He preened a feather crest with three fingers. 'And through knowing you, perhaps I have tempered the pride which rules my world.' He nodded to himself. 'I, too, will remain silent.' A subtle Vegan smile flitted across his face, disappeared.

Trent recalled the beagle head he had seen under the parachute when he'd recovered consciousness. 'I'd like to see one of these animals.'

'That can be . . .' Ger was interrupted by the near baying of a pack of hounds. He stood up, flung open the window louvres, returned to support Trent's head. 'Look out there, friend Varley.'

On the blue-green Vegan plain, Trent could see a pack of hounds coursing in pursuit of a herd of runaway *ichikas*. The hounds had the familiar beagle head, brown and white fur. All had six legs.

PASSAGE FOR PIANO

Had some cosmic crystal gazer suggested to Margaret Hatchell that she would try to smuggle a concert grand piano onto the colony spaceship, she would have been shocked. Here she was at home in her kitchen on a hot summer afternoon, worried about how to squeeze *ounces* into her family's meager weight allowance for the trip – and the piano weighed more than half a *ton*.

Before she had married Walter Hatchell, she had been a working nurse-dietician, which made her of some use to the colony group destined for Planet C. But Walter, as the expedition's chief ecologist, was one of the most important cogs in the effort. His field was bionomics: the science of setting up the delicate balance of growing things to support human life on an alien world.

Walter was tied to his work at the White Sands base, hadn't been home to Seattle for a month during this crucial preparation period. This left Margaret with two children and several problems – the chief problem being that one of their children was a blind piano prodigy subject to black moods.

Margaret glanced at the clock on her kitchen wall: three-thirty, time to start dinner. She wheeled the microfilming cabinet out of her kitchen and down the hall to the music room to get it out of her way. Coming into the familiar music room, she suddenly felt herself a hesitant stranger here – almost afraid to look too closely at her favorite wing-back chair, or at her son's concert grand piano, or at the rose pattern rug with afternoon sun streaming dappled gold across it.

It was a sensation of unreality – something like the feeling that had caught her the day the colonization board had notified them that the Hatchells had been chosen.

'We're going to be pioneers on Planet C,' she whispered.

But that made it no more real. She wondered if others among the three hundred and eight chosen colonists felt the same way about moving to a virgin world.

In the first days after the selection, when they all had been assembled at White Sands for preliminary instructions, a young astronomer had given a brief lecture.

'Your sun will be the star Giansar,' he had said, and his voice had echoed in the barnlike hall as he pointed to the star on the chart. 'In the tail of constellation Dragon. Your ship will travel sixteen years on sub-macro drive to make the passage from Earth. You already know, of course, that you will pass this time in sleep-freeze, and it'll feel just like one night to you. Giansar has a more orange light than our sun, and it's somewhat cooler. However, Planet C is closer to its sun, and this means your climate will average out warmer than we experience here.'

Margaret had tried to follow the astronomer's words closely, just as she had done in the other lectures, but only the high points remained from all of them: orange light, warmer climate, less moisture, conserve weight in what you take along, seventy-five pounds of private luggage allowed for each adult, forty pounds for children to age fourteen . . .

Now, standing in her music room, Margaret felt that it must have been some other person who had listened to those lectures. *I should be excited and happy*, she thought. *Why do I feel so sad?*

At thirty-five, Margaret Hatchell looked an indeterminate mid-twenty with a good figure, a graceful walk. Her brown hair carried reddish lights. The dark eyes, full mouth and firm chin combined to give an impression of hidden fire.

She rubbed a hand along the curved edge of the piano lid, felt the dent where the instrument had hit the door when they'd moved here to Seattle from Denver. *How long ago?* she asked herself. *Eight years? Yes . . . it was the year after Grandfather Maurice Hatchell died . . . after playing his final concert with this very piano.*

Through the open back windows she could hear her

nine-year-old, Rita, filling the summer afternoon with a *discussion* of the strange insects to be discovered on Planet C. Rita's audience consisted of non-colonist playmates overawed by the fame of their companion. Rita was referring to their colony world as 'Ritelle,' the name she had submitted to the Survey and Exploration Service.

Margaret thought: *If they choose Rita's name we'll never hear the end of it . . . literally!*

Realization that an entire planet could be named for her daughter sent Margaret's thoughts reeling off on a new tangent. She stood silently in the golden shadows of the music room, one hand on the piano that had belonged to her husband's father, Maurice Hatchell – *the* Maurice Hatchell of concert fame. For the first time, Margaret saw something of what the news service people had been telling her just that morning – that her family and all the other colonists were 'chosen people,' and for this reason their lives were of tremendous interest to everyone on Earth.

She noted her son's bat-eye radar box and its shoulder harness atop the piano. That meant David was somewhere around the house. He never used the box in the familiarity of his home where memory served in place of the sight he had lost. Seeing the box there prompted Margaret to move the microfilming cabinet aside where David would not trip over it if he came to the music room to practice. She listened, wondering if David was upstairs trying the lightweight electronic piano that had been built for him to take on the spaceship. There was no hint of his music in the soft sounds of the afternoon, but then he could have turned the sound low.

Thinking of David brought to her mind the boy's tantrum that had ended the news-film session just before lunch. The chief reporter – *What was his name? Bonaudi?* – had asked how they intended to dispose of the concert grand piano. She could still hear the awful discord as David had crashed his fists onto the keyboard. He had leaped up, dashed from the room – a dark little figure full of impotent fury.

Twelve is such an emotional age, she told herself.

Margaret decided that her sadness was the same as David's. *It's the parting with beloved possessions . . . it's the certain knowledge that we'll never see these things again . . . that all we'll have will be films and lightweight substitutes.* A sensation of terrible longing filled her. *Never again to feel the homely comfort of so many things that spell family tradition: the wing-back chair Walter and I bought when we furnished our first house, the sewing cabinet that great-great grandmother Chrisman brought from Ohio, the oversize double bed built specially to accommodate Walter's long frame . . .*

Abruptly, she turned away from the piano, went back to the kitchen. It was a white tile room with black fixtures, a laboratory kitchen cluttered now with debris of packing. Margaret pushed aside her recipe files on the counter beside the sink, being careful not to disturb the yellow scrap of paper that marked where she'd stopped microfilming them. The sink was still piled with her mother's Spode china that was being readied for the space journey. Cups and saucers would weigh three and a half pounds in their special packing. Margaret resumed washing the dishes, seating them in the delicate webs of the lightweight box.

The wall phone beside her came alive to the operator's face. 'Hatchell residence?'

Margaret lifted her dripping hands from the sink, nudged the call switch with her elbow. 'Yes?'

'On your call to Walter Hatchell at White Sands: he still is not available. Shall I try again in twenty minutes?'

'Please do.'

The operator's face faded from the screen. Margaret nudged off the switch, resumed washing. The newsfilm group had shot several pictures of her working at the sink that morning. She wondered how she and her family would appear on the film. The reporter had called Rita a 'budding entomologist' and had referred to David as 'the blind piano prodigy – one of the few victims of the *drum* virus brought back from the uninhabitable Planet A-4.'

Rita came in from the yard. She was a lanky nine-year-old, a precocious extrovert with large blue eyes that looked on the world as her own private problem waiting to be solved.

'I am desperately ravenous,' she announced. 'When do we eat?'

'When it's ready,' Margaret said. She noted with a twinge of exasperation that Rita had acquired a torn cobweb on her blonde hair and a smudge of dirt across her left cheek.

Why should a little girl be fascinated by bugs? Margaret asked herself. *It's not natural.* She said: 'How'd you get the cobweb in your hair?'

'Oh, succotash!' Rita put a hand to her hair, rubbed away the offending web.

'How?' repeated Margaret.

'Mother! If one is to acquire knowledge of the insect world, one inevitably encounters such things! I am just dismayed that I tore the web.'

'Well, I'm dismayed that you're filthy dirty. Go upstairs and wash so you'll look presentable when we get the call through to your father.'

Rita turned away.

'And weigh yourself,' called Margaret. 'I have to turn in our family's weekly weight aggregate tomorrow.'

Rita skipped out of the room.

Margaret felt certain she had heard a muttered 'parents!' The sound of the child's footsteps diminished up the stairs. A door slammed on the second floor. Presently, Rita clattered back down the stairs. She ran into the kitchen. 'Mother, you . . .'

'You haven't had time to get clean.' Margaret spoke without turning.

'It's David,' said Rita. 'He looks peculiar and he says he doesn't want any supper.'

Margaret turned from the sink, her features set to hide the gripping of fear. She knew from experience that Rita's 'peculiar' could be anything . . . literally anything.

'How do you mean *peculiar*, dear?'

'He's so pale. He looks like he doesn't have any blood.'

For some reason, this brought to Margaret's mind a memory picture of David at the age of three – a still figure in a hospital bed, flesh-colored feeding tube protruding from his nose, and his skin as pale as death with his breathing so quiet it was difficult to detect the chest movements.

She dried her hands on a dishtowel. 'Let's go have a look. He's probably just tired.'

David was stretched out on his bed, one arm thrown across his eyes. The shades were drawn and the room was in semi-darkness. It took a moment for Margaret's eyes to adjust to the gloom, and she thought: *Do the blind seek darkness because it gives them the advantage over those with sight?* She crossed to the bedside. The boy was a small, dark-haired figure – his father's coloring. The chin was narrow and the mouth a firm line like his grandfather Hatchell's. Right now he looked thin and defenseless . . . and Rita was right: terribly pale.

Margaret adopted her best hospital manner, lifted David's arm from his face, took his pulse.

'Don't you feel well, Davey?' she asked.

'I wish you wouldn't call me that,' he said. 'That's a baby name.' His narrow features were set, sullen.

She took a short, quick breath. 'Sorry. I forgot. Rita says you don't want any supper.'

Rita came in from the hallway. 'He looks positively infirm, mother.'

'Does she have to keep pestering me?' demanded David.

'I thought I heard the phone chime,' said Margaret. 'Will you go check, Rita?'

'You're being offensively obvious,' said Rita. 'If you don't want me in here, just say so.' She turned, walked slowly out of the room.

'Do you hurt someplace, David?' asked Margaret.

'I just feel tired,' he muttered. 'Why can't you leave me alone?'

Margaret stared down at him – caught as she had been

so many times by his resemblance to his grandfather Hatchell. It was a resemblance made uncanny when the boy sat down at the piano: that same intense vibrancy . . . the same musical genius that had made Hatchell a name to fill concert halls. And she thought: *Perhaps it's because the Steinway belonged to his grandfather that he feels so badly about parting with it. The piano's a symbol of the talent he inherited.*

She patted her son's hand, sat down beside him on the bed. 'Is something troubling you, David?'

His features contorted, and he whirled away from her. 'Go away!' He muttered. 'Just leave me alone!'

Margaret sighed, felt inadequate. She wished desperately that Walter were not tied to the work at the launching site. She felt a deep need of her husband at this moment. Another sigh escaped her. She knew what she had to do. The rules for colonists were explicit: any symptoms at all – even superficial ones – were to get a doctor's attention. She gave David's hand a final pat, went downstairs to the hall phone, called Dr Mowery, the medic cleared for colonists in the Seattle area. He said he'd be out in about an hour.

Rita came in as Margaret was completing the call, asked: 'Is David going to die?'

All the tenseness and aggravation of the day came out in Margaret's reply: 'Don't be such a beastly little fool!'

Immediately, she was sorry. She stooped, gathered Rita to her, crooned apologies.

'It's all right, mother,' Rita said. 'I realize you're overwrought.'

Filled with contriteness, Margaret went into the kitchen, prepared her daughter's favorite food: tunafish sandwiches and chocolate milkshakes.

I'm getting too jumpy, thought Margaret. *David's not really sick. It's the hot weather we've had lately and all this tension of getting ready to go.* She took a sandwich and milkshake up to the boy, but he still refused to eat. And there was such a pallid sense of defeat about him. A story about someone who had died merely because he gave up the will to live entered her mind and refused to be shaken.

She made her way back down to the kitchen, dabbled at the work there until the call to Walter went through. Her husband's craggy features and deep voice brought the calmness she had been seeking all day.

'I miss you so much, darling,' she said.

'It won't be much longer,' he said. He smiled, leaned to one side, exposing the impersonal wall of a pay booth behind him. He looked tired. 'How's my family?'

She told him about David, saw the worry creep into his eyes. 'Is the doctor there yet?' he asked.

'He's late. He should've been here by six and it's half past.'

'Probably busy as a bird dog,' he said. 'It doesn't really sound as though David's actually sick. Just upset more likely . . . the excitement of leaving. Call me as soon as the doctor tells you what's wrong.'

'I will. I think he's just upset over leaving your father's piano behind.'

'David knows it's not that we want to leave these things.' A grin brightened his features. 'Lord! Imagine taking that thing on the ship! Dr Charlesworthy would flip!'

She smiled. 'Why don't you suggest it.'

'You're trying to get me in trouble with the old man!'

'How're things going, dear?' she asked.

His face sobered. He sighed. 'I had to talk to poor Smythe's widow today. She came out to pick up his things. It was rather trying. The old man was afraid she might still want to come along . . . but no . . .' He shook his head.

'Do you have his replacement yet?'

'Yes. Young fellow from Lebanon. Name's Teryk. His wife's a cute little thing.' Walter looked past her at the kitchen.' Looks like you're getting things in order. Decided yet what you're taking?'

'Some of the things. I wish I could make decisions like you do. I've definitely decided to take mother's Spode china cups and saucers and sterling silver . . . for Rita when she gets married . . . and the Utrillo your father bought in Lisbon . . . and I've weeded my jewelry down to about two pounds of basics . . . and I'm not going to worry about cosmetics since you say we can make our own when we . . .'

Rita ran into the kitchen, pushed in beside Margaret. 'Hello, father.'

'Hi, punkin head. What've you been up to?'

'I've been cataloging my insect collection and filling it out. Mother's going to help me film the glassed-in specimens as soon as I'm ready. They're so *heavy*!'

'How'd you wangle her agreement to get that close to your bugs?'

'Father! They're not bugs; they're entomological specimens.'

'They're bugs to your mother, honey. Now, if . . .'

'Father! There's one other thing. I told Raul – he's the new boy down the block – I told him today about those hawklike insects on Ritelle that . . .'

'They're not insects, honey; they're adapted amphibians.'

She frowned. 'But Spencer's report distinctly says that they're chitinous and they . . .'

'Whoa down! You should've read the technical report, the one I showed you when I was home last month. These critters have a copper-base metabolism, and they're closely allied to a common fish on the planet.'

'Oh . . . Do you think I'd better branch out into marine biology?'

'One thing at a time, honey. Now . . .'

'Have we set the departure date yet, father? I can hardly wait to get to work there.'

'It's not definite yet, honey. But we should know any day. Now, let me talk to your mother.'

Rita pulled back.

Walter smiled at his wife. 'What're we raising there?'

'I wish I knew.'

'Look . . . don't worry about David. It's been nine years

since . . . since he recovered from that virus. All the tests show that he was completely cured.'

And she thought: *Yes . . . cured – except for the little detail of no optic nerves.* She forced a smile. 'I know you're probably right. It'll turn out to be something simple . . . and we'll laugh about this when . . .' The front doorbell chimed. 'That's probably the doctor now.'

'Call me when you find out,' said Walter.

Margaret heard Rita's footsteps running toward the door.

'I'll sign off, sweet,' she said. She blew a kiss to her husband. 'I love you.'

Walter held up two fingers in a victory sign, winked. 'Same here. Chin up.'

They broke the connection.

Dr Mowery was a gray-haired, flint-faced bustler – addicted to the nodding head and the knowing (but unintelligible) murmur. One big hand held a gray instrument bag. He had a pat on the head for Rita, a firm handshake for Margaret, and he insisted on seeing David alone.

'Mothers just clutter up the atmosphere for a doctor,' he said, and he winked to take the sting from his words.

Margaret sent Rita to her room, waited in the upstairs hall. There were one hundred and six flower panels on the wallpaper between the door to David's room and the corner of the hall. She was moving on to count the rungs in the balustrade when the doctor emerged from David's room. He closed the door softly behind him, nodding to himself.

She waited.

'Mmmmmm-hmmmmm,' said Dr Mowery. He cleared his throat.

'Is it anything serious?' asked Margaret.

'Not sure.' He walked to the head of the stairs. 'How long's the boy been acting like that . . . listless and upset?'

Margaret swallowed a lump in her throat. 'He's been acting differently ever since they delivered the electronic piano . . . the one that's going to substitute for his grand-father's Steinway. Is that what you mean?'

'Differently?'

'Rebellious, short-tempered . . . wanting to be alone.'

'I suppose there's not the remotest possibility of his taking the big piano,' said the doctor.

'Oh, my goodness . . . it must weigh all of a thousand pounds,' said Margaret. 'The electronic instrument is only twenty-one pounds.' She cleared her throat. 'Is it worry about the piano, doctor?'

'Possibly.' Dr Mowery nodded, took the first step down the stairs. 'It doesn't appear to be anything organic that my instruments can find. I'm going to have Dr Linquist and some others look in on David tonight. Dr Linquist is our chief psychiatrist. Meanwhile, I'd try to get the boy to eat something.'

She crossed to Dr Mowery's side at the head of the stairs. 'I'm a nurse,' she said. 'You can tell me if it's something serious that . . .'

He shifted his bag to his right hand, patted her arm. 'Now don't you worry, my dear. The colonization group is fortunate to have a musical genius in its roster. We're not going to let anything happen to him.'

Dr Linquist had the round face and cynical eyes of a fallen cherub. His voice surged out of him in waves that flowed over the listener and towed him under. The psychiatrist and colleagues were with David until almost ten pm. Then Dr Linquist dismissed the others, came down to the music room where Margaret was waiting. He sat on the piano bench, hands gripping the lip of wood beside him.

Margaret occupied her wing-back chair – the one piece of furniture she knew she would miss more than any other thing in the house. Long usage had worn contours in the chair that exactly complemented her, and its rough fabric upholstery held the soothing texture of familiarity.

The night outside the screened windows carried a sonorous sawing of crickets.

'We can say definitely that it's a fixation about this piano,' said Linquist. He slapped his palms onto his knees. 'Have you ever thought of leaving the boy behind?'

'Doctor!'

'Thought I'd ask.'

'Is it *that* serious with Davey?' she asked. 'I mean, after all . . . we're all of us going to miss things.' She rubbed the chair arm. 'But good heavens, we . . .'

'I'm not much of a musician,' said Linquist. 'I'm told by the critics, though, that your boy already has concert stature . . . that he's being deliberately held back now to avoid piling confusion on confusion . . . I mean with your leaving so soon and all.' The psychiatrist tugged at his lower lip. 'You realize, of course, that your boy worships the memory of his grandfather?'

'He's seen all the old stereos, listened to all the tapes,' said Margaret. 'He was only four when grandfather died, but David remembers everything they ever did together. It was . . .' She shrugged.

'David has identified his inherited talent with his inherited piano,' said Linquist. 'He . . .'

'But pianos can be replaced,' said Margaret. 'Couldn't one of our colony carpenters or cabinetmakers duplicate . . .'

'Ah, no,' said Linquist. 'Not duplicate. It would not be the piano of Maurice Hatchell. You see, your boy is overly conscious that he inherited musical genius from his grandfather . . . just as he inherited the piano. He's tied the two together. He believes that if – not consciously, you understand? But he believes, nonetheless, that if he loses the piano he loses the talent. And there you have a problem more critical than you might suspect.'

She shook her head. 'But children get over these . . .'

'He's not a child, Mrs Hatchell. Perhaps I should say he's not *just* a child. He is that sensitive thing we call *genius*. This is a delicate state that goes sour all too easily.'

She felt her mouth go dry. 'What are you trying to tell me?'

'I don't want to alarm you without cause, Mrs Hatchell. But the truth is – and this is the opinion of all of us – that if your boy is deprived of his musical outlet . . . well, he could die.'

She paled. 'Oh, no! He . . .'

'Such things happen, Mrs Hatchell. There are therapeutic procedures we could use, of course, but I'm not sure we have the time. They're expecting to set your departure date momentarily. Therapy *could* take years.'

'But David's . . .'

'David is precocious and over emotional,' said Linquist. 'He's invested much more than is healthy in his music. His blindness accounts for part of that, but over and above the fact of blindness there's his need for musical expression. In a genius such as David this is akin to one of the basic drives of life itself.'

'We couldn't leave him,' she whispered. 'We just couldn't. You don't understand. We're such a close family that we . . .'

'Then perhaps you should step aside, let some other family have your . . .'

'It would kill Walter . . . my husband,' she said. 'He's lived for this chance.' She shook her head. 'Anyway, I'm not sure we could back out now. Walter's assistant, Dr Smythe, was killed in a 'copter crash near Phoenix last week. They already have a replacement, but I'm sure you know how important Walter's function is to the colony's success.'

Linquist nodded. 'I read about Smythe, but I failed to make the obvious association here.'

'I'm not important to the colony,' she said. 'Nor the children, really. But the ecologists – the success of our entire effort hangs on them. Without Walter . . .'

'We'll just have to solve it then,' he said. He got to his feet. 'We'll be back tomorrow for another look at David, Mrs Hatchell. Dr Mowery made him take some amino pills and then gave him a sedative. He should sleep right through the night. If there're any complications – although there shouldn't be – you can reach me at this number.' He pulled a card from his wallet, gave it to her. 'It is too bad about the weight problem. I'm sure it would solve everything if he could just take this monster with him.' Linquist patted the piano lid. 'Well . . . good night.'

When Linquist had gone, Margaret leaned against the front door, pressed her forehead against the cool wood. 'No,' she whispered. 'No . . . no . . . no . . .' Presently, she went to the living room phone, placed a call to Walter. It was ten twenty pm. The call went right through, proving that he had been waiting for it. Margaret noted the deep worry creases in her husband's forehead, longed to reach out, touch them, smooth them.

'What is it, Margaret?' he asked. 'Is David all right?'

'Dear, it's . . .' she swallowed. 'It's about the piano. Your father's Steinway.'

'The *piano*?'

'The doctors have been here all evening up to a few minutes ago examining David. The psychiatrist says if David loses the piano he may lose his . . . his music . . . his . . . and if he loses that he could die.'

Walter blinked. 'Over a piano? Oh, now, surely there must be some . . .'

She told him everything Dr Linquist had said.

'The boy's so much like dad,' said Walter. 'Dad once threw the philharmonic into an uproar because his piano bench was a half inch too low. Good Lord! I . . . What'd Linquist say we could do?'

'He said if we could take the piano it'd solve . . .'

'That concert grand? The damn' thing must weigh over a thousand pounds. That's more than three times what our whole family is allowed in private luggage.'

'I know. I'm almost at my wits' ends. All this turmoil of deciding what's to go and now . . . David.'

'To go!' barked Walter. 'Good Lord! What with worrying about David I almost forgot: our departure date was set just tonight.' He glanced at his watch. 'Blast off is fourteen days and six hours away – give or take a few minutes. The old man said . . .'

'Fourteen days!'

'Yes, but *you* have only eight days. That's the colony assembly date. The pickup crews will be around to get your luggage on the afternoon of . . .'

'Walter! I haven't even decided what to . . .' She broke off. 'I was sure we had at least another month. You told me yourself that we . . .'

'I know. But fuel production came out ahead of schedule, and the long range weather forecast is favorable. And it's part of the psychology not to drag out leave taking. This way the shock of abruptness cuts everything clean.'

'But what're we going to do about David?' She chewed her lower lip.

'Is he awake?'

'I don't think so. They gave him a sedative.'

Walter frowned. 'I want to talk to David first thing in the morning. I've been neglecting him lately because of all the work here, but . . .'

'He understands, Walter.'

'I'm sure he does, but I want to see him for myself. I only wish I had the time to come home, but things are pretty frantic here right now.' He shook his head. 'I just don't see how that diagnosis could be right. All this fuss over a piano!'

'Walter . . . you're not attached to things. With you it's people and ideas.' She lowered her eyes, fought back tears. 'But some people can grow to love inanimate objects, too . . . things that mean comfort and security.' She swallowed.

He shook his head. 'I guess I just don't understand. We'll work out something, though. Depend on it.'

Margaret forced a smile. 'I know you will, dear.'

'Now that we have the departure date it may blow the whole thing right out of his mind,' Walter said.

'Perhaps you're right.'

He glanced at his wristwatch. 'I have to sign off now.

Got some experiments running.' He winked. 'I miss my family.'

'So do I,' she whispered.

In the morning there was a call from Prester Charlesworthy, colony director. His face came onto the phone screen in Margaret's kitchen just as she finished dishing up breakfast for Rita. David was still in bed. And Margaret had told neither of them about the departure date.

Charlesworthy was a man of skinny features, nervous mannerisms. There was a bumpkin look about him until you saw the incisive stare of the pale blue eyes.

'Forgive me for bothering you like this, Mrs Hatchell,' he said.

She forced herself to calmness. 'No bother. We were expecting a call from Walter this morning. I thought this was it.'

'I've just been talking to Walter,' said Charlesworthy. 'He's been telling me about David. We had a report first thing this morning from Dr Linquist.'

After a sleepless night with periodic cat-footed trips to look in on David, Margaret felt her nerves jangling out to frayed helplessness. She was primed to leap at the worst interpretations that entered her mind. 'You're putting us out of the colony group!' she blurted. 'You're getting another ecologist to . . .'

'Oh, no, Mrs Hatchell!' Dr Charlesworthy took a deep breath. 'I know it must seem odd – my calling you like this – but our little group will be alone on a very alien world, very dependent upon each other for almost ten years . . . until the next ship gets there. We've got to work together on everything. I sincerely want to help you.'

'I'm sorry,' she said. 'But I didn't get much sleep last night.'

'I quite understand. Believe me, I'd like nothing better than to be able to send Walter home to you right now.' Charlesworthy shrugged. 'But that's out of the question. With poor Smythe dead there's a terribly heavy load on

Walter's shoulders. Without him, we might even have to abort this attempt.'

Margaret wet her lips with her tongue. 'Dr Charlesworthy, is there any possibility at all that we could . . . I mean . . . the piano – take it on the ship?'

'Mrs Hatchell!' Charlesworthy pulled back from his screen. 'It must weigh half a ton!' .

' She sighed. 'I called the moving company first thing this morning – the company that moved the piano here into this house. They checked their records. It weighs fourteen hundred and eight pounds.'

'Out of the question! Why . . . we've had to eliminate high priority technical equipment that doesn't weigh half that much!'

'I guess I'm desperate,' she said. 'I keep thinking over what Dr Linquist said about David dying if . . .'

'Of course,' said Charlesworthy. 'That's why I called you. I want you to know what we've done. We dispatched Hector Torres to the Steinway factory this morning. Hector is one of the cabinetmakers we'll have in the colony. The Steinway people have generously consented to show him all of their construction secrets so Hector can build an exact duplicate of this piano – correct in all details. Philip Jackson, one of our metallurgists, will be following Hector this afternoon for the same reason. I'm sure that when you tell David this it'll completely resolve all his fears.'

Margaret blinked back tears. 'Dr Charlesworthy . . . I don't know how to thank you.'

'Don't thank me at all, my dear. We're a team . . . we pull together.' He nodded. 'Now, one other thing: a favor you can do for me.'

'Certainly.'

'Try not to worry Walter too much this week if you can. He's discovered a mutation that may permit us to cross earth plants with ones already growing on Planet C. He's running final tests this week with dirt samples from C. These are crucial tests, Mrs Hatchell. They could cut several years off the initial stage of setting up a new life-cycle balance.'

'Of course,' she said. 'I'm sorry that I . . .'

'Don't you be sorry. And don't you worry. The boy's only twelve. Time heals all things.'

'I'm sure it'll work out,' she said.

'Excellent,' said Charlesworthy. 'That's the spirit. Now, you call on me for any help you may need . . . day or night. We're a team. We have to pull together.'

They broke the connection. Margaret stood in front of the phone, facing the blank screen.

Rita spoke from the kitchen table behind her. 'What'd he say about the departure date?'

'It's been set, dear,' Margaret turned. 'We have to be with Daddy at White Sands in eight days.'

'Whooopeee!' Rita leaped to her feet, upsetting her breakfast dishes. 'We're going! We're going!'

'Rita!'

But Rita already was dashing out of the room, out of the house. Her 'Eight days!' echoed back from the front hall.

Margaret stepped to the kitchen door. 'Rita!'

Her daughter ran back down the hall. 'I'm going to tell the kids!'

'You will calm down right now. You're making enough noise to . . .'

'I heard her.' It was David at the head of the stairs. He came down slowly, guiding himself by the bannister. His face looked white as eggshell, and there was a dragging hesitancy to his steps.

Margaret took a deep breath, told him about Dr Charlesworthy's plan to replace the piano.

David stopped two steps above her, head down. When she had finished, he said: 'It won't be the same.' He stepped around her, went into the music room. There was a slumped finality to his figure.

Margaret whirled back into the kitchen. Angry determination flamed in her. She heard Rita's slow footsteps following, spoke without turning: 'Rita, how much weight can you cut from your luggage?'

'Mother!'

'We're going to take that piano!' snapped Margaret.

Rita came up beside her. 'But our whole family gets to take only two hundred and thirty pounds! We couldn't possibly . . .'

'There are three hundred and eight of us in this colonization group,' said Margaret. 'Every adult is allowed seventy-five pounds, every child under fourteen years gets forty pounds.' She found her kitchen scratch pad, scribbled figures on it. 'If each person donates only four pounds and twelve ounces we can take that piano!' Before she could change her mind, she whirled to the drainboard, swept the package with her mother's Spode china cups and saucers into the discard box. 'There! A gift for the people who bought our house! And that's three and a half pounds of it!'

Then she began to cry.

Rita sobered. 'I'll leave my insect specimens,' she whispered. Then she buried her head in her mother's dress, and she too was sobbing.

'What're you two crying about?' David spoke from the kitchen doorway, his bat-eye box strapped to his shoulders. His small features were drawn into a pinched look of misery.

Margaret dried her eyes. 'Davey . . . David, we're going to try to take your piano with us.'

His chin lifted, his features momentarily relaxed, then the tight unhappiness returned. 'Sure. They'll just dump out some of dad's seeds and a few tools and scientific instruments for my . . .'

'There's another way,' she said.

'What other way?' His voice was fighting against a hope that might be smashed.

Margaret explained her plan.

'Go begging?' he asked. 'Asking people to give up their own . . .'

'David, this will be a barren and cold new world we're going to colonize – very few comforts, drab issue clothing – almost no refinements or the things we think of as belonging to a civilized culture. A real honest to goodness earth piano and the . . . man to play it would help. It'd help our morale, and keep down the homesickness that's sure to come.'

His sightless eyes appeared to stare at her for a long moment of silence; then he said: 'That would be a terrible responsibility for me.'

She felt pride in her son flow all through her, said: 'I'm glad you see it that way.'

The small booklet of regulations and advice handed out at the first assembly in White Sands carried names and addresses of all the colonists. Margaret started at the top of the list, called Selma Atkins of Little Rock, wife of the expedition's head zoologist.

Mrs Atkins was a dark little button of a woman with flaming hair and a fizzing personality. She turned out to be a born conspirator. Before Margaret had finished explaining the problem, Selma Atkins was volunteering to head a phone committee. She jotted down names of prospects, said: 'Even if we get the weight allowance, how'll we get the thing aboard?'

Margaret looked puzzled. 'What's wrong with just showing that we have the weight allowance, and handing the piano over to the people who pack things on the ship?'

'Charlesworthy'd never go for it, honey. He's livid at the amount of equipment that's had to be passed over because of the weight problem. He'd take one look at one thousand four hundred and eight pounds of piano and say: "That'll be a spare atomic generation kit!" My husband says he's had to drill holes in packing boxes to save ounces!'

'But how could we smuggle . . .'

Selma snapped her fingers. 'I know! Ozzy Lucan!'

'Lucan?'

'The ship's steward,' said Selma. 'You know: the big

horse of a man with red hair. He spoke at one of the meetings on – you know – all about how to conserve weight in packing and how to use the special containers.'

'Oh, yes,' said Margaret. 'What about him?'

'He's married to my third cousin Betty's oldest daughter. Nothing like a little family pressure. I'll work on it.'

'Wouldn't he be likely to go directly to Charlesworthy with it?' asked Margaret.

'Hah!' barked Selma. 'You don't know Betty's side of our family!'

Dr Linquist arrived in the middle of the morning, two consultant psychiatrists in tow. They spent an hour with David, came down to the kitchen where Margaret and Rita were finishing the microfilming of the recipe files. David followed them, stood in the doorway.

'The boy's apparently tougher than I realized,' said Linquist. 'Are you sure he hasn't been told he can take that piano? I hope you haven't been misleading him to make him feel better.'

David frowned.

Margaret said: 'Dr Charlesworthy refused to take the piano when I asked him. However, he's sent two experts to the Steinway factory so we'll be sure of an exact duplicate.'

Linquist turned to David. 'And that's all right with you, David?'

David hesitated, then: 'I understand about the weight.'

'Well, I guess you're growing up,' said Linquist.

When the psychiatrists had gone, Rita turned on Margaret. 'Mother! You lied to them!'

'No she didn't,' said David. 'She told the exact truth.'

'But not all of it,' said Margaret.

'That's just the same as lying,' said Rita.

'Oh, stop it!' snapped Margaret. Then: 'David, are you sure you want to leave your braille texts?'

'Yes. That's sixteen pounds. We've got the braille punch kit and the braille typewriter; I can type new copies of everything I'll need if Rita will read to me.'

By three o'clock that afternoon they had Chief Steward Oswald Lucan's reluctant agreement to smuggle the piano aboard if they could get the weight allowance precise to the ounce. But Lucan's parting words were: 'Don't let the old man get wind of this. He's boiling about the equipment we've had to cut out.'

At seven-thirty, Margaret added the first day's weight donations: sixty-one commitments for a total of two hundred and seven pounds and seven ounces. *Not enough from each person*, she told herself. *But I can't blame them. We're all tied to our possessions. It's so hard to part with all the little things that link us with the past and with Earth. We've got to find more weight somewhere.* She cast about in her own mind for things to discard, knew a sense of futility at the few pounds she had at her disposal.

By ten o'clock on the morning of the third day they had five hundred and fifty-four pounds and eight ounces from one hundred and sixty of their fellow colonists. They also had an even twenty violent rejections. The tension of fear that one of these twenty might give away their conspiracy was beginning to tell on Margaret.

David, too, was sinking back into gloom. He sat on the piano bench in the music room, Margaret behind him in her favorite chair. One of David's hands absently caressed the keys that Maurice Hatchell had brought to such crashing life.

'We're getting less than four pounds per person, aren't we?' asked David.

Margaret rubbed her cheek. 'Yes.'

A gentle chord came from the piano. 'We aren't going to make it,' said David. A fluid rippling of music lifted in the room. 'I'm not sure we have the right to ask this of people anyway. They're giving up so much already, and then we . . .'

'Hush, Davey.'

He let the baby name pass, coaxed a floating passage of Debussy from the keys.

Margaret put her hands to her eyes, cried silently with

fatigue and frustration. But the tears coming from David's fingers on the piano went deeper.

Presently, he stood up, walked slowly out of the room, up the stairs. She heard his bedroom door close softly. The lack of violence in his actions cut her like a knife.

The phone chime broke Margaret from her blue reverie. She took the call on the portable in the hall. Selma Atkins' features came onto the screen, wide-eyed, subdued.

'Ozzy just called me,' she blurted. 'Somebody snitched to Charlesworthy this morning.'

Margaret put a hand over her mouth.

'Did you tell your husband what we were doing?' asked Selma.

'No.' Margaret shook her head. 'I was going to, and then I got afraid of what he'd say. He and Charlesworthy are very close friends, you know.'

'You mean he'd peach on his own wife?'

'Oh, no, but he might . . .'

'Well, he's on the carpet now,' said Selma. 'Ozzy says the whole base is jumping. He was shouting and banging his hands on the desk at Walter and . . .'

'Charlesworthy?'

'Who else? I called to warn you. He . . .'

'But what'll we do?' asked Margaret.

'We run for cover, honey. We fall back and regroup. Call me as soon as you've talked to him. Maybe we can think of a new plan.'

'We've contributions from more than half the colonists,' said Margaret. 'That means we've more than half of them on our side to begin . . .'

'Right now the colony organization is a dictatorship, not a democracy,' said Selma. 'But I'll be thinking about it. Bye now.'

David came up behind her as she was breaking the connection. 'I heard,' he said. 'That finishes us, doesn't it?'

The phone chimed before she could answer him. She flipped the switch. Walter's face came onto the screen. He looked haggard, the craggy lines more pronounced.

'Margaret,' he said. 'I'm calling from Dr Charlesworthy's office.' He took a deep breath. 'Why didn't you come to me about this? I could've told you how foolish it was!'

'That's why!' she said.

'But smuggling a piano onto the ship! Of all the . . .'

'I was thinking of Davey!' she snapped.

'Good Lord, I know it! But . . .'

'When the doctors said he might die if he lost his . . .'

'But Margaret, a thousand-pound piano!'

'Fourteen hundred and eight pounds,' she corrected him.

'Let's not argue, darling,' he said. 'I admire your guts . . . and I love you, but I can't let you endanger the social solidarity of the colony group . . .' he shook his head '. . . not even for David.'

'Even if it kills your own son?' she demanded.

'I'm not about to kill my son,' he said. 'I'm an ecologist, remember? It's my job to keep us alive . . . as a group *and* singly! And I . . .'

'Dad's right,' said David. He moved up beside Margaret.

'I didn't know you were there, son,' said Walter.

'It's all right, Dad.'

'Just a moment, please.' It was Charlesworthy, pushing in beside Walter. 'I want to know how much weight allowance you've been promised.'

'Why?' asked Margaret. 'So you can figure how many more scientific *toys* to take along?'

'I want to know how close you are to success in your little project,' he said.

'Five hundred and fifty-four pounds and eight ounces,' she said. 'Contributions from one hundred and sixty people!'

Charlesworthy pursed his lips. 'Just about one-third of what you need,' he said. 'And at this rate you wouldn't get enough. If you had any chance of success I'd almost be inclined to say go ahead, but you can see for yourself that . . .'

'I have an idea,' said David.

Charlesworthy looked at him. 'You're David?'

'Yes, sir.'

'What's your idea?'

'How much would the harp and keyboard from my piano weigh? You have people at the factory . . .'

'You mean take just that much of your piano?' asked Charlesworthy.

'Yes, sir. It wouldn't be the same . . . it'd be better. It would have roots in both worlds – part of the piano from Earth and part from Planet C.'

'Darned if I don't like the idea,' said Charlesworthy. He turned. 'Walter, call Phil Jackson at the Steinway plant. Find out how much that portion of the piano would weigh.'

Walter left the field of the screen. The others waited. Presently, Walter returned, said: 'Five hundred and sixty-two pounds more or less. Hector Torres was on the line, too. He said he's sure he can duplicate the rest of the piano exactly.'

Charlesworthy smiled. 'That's it, then! I'm out of my mind . . . we need so many other things with us so desperately. But maybe we need this too: for morale.'

'With the right morale we can make anything else we may need,' said Walter.

Margaret found a scratch pad in the phone drawer, scribbled figures on it. She looked up: 'I'll get busy right now and find a way to meet the extra few pounds we'll need to . . .'

'How much more?' asked Charlesworthy.

Margaret looked down at her scratch pad. 'Seven pounds and eight ounces.'

Charlesworthy took a deep breath. 'While I'm still out of my mind, let me make another gesture: Mrs Charlesworthy and I will contribute seven pounds and eight ounces to the cultural future of our new home.'

ENCOUNTER IN A LONELY PLACE

'You're interested in extrasensory perception, eh? Well, I guess I've seen as much of that as the next fellow and that's no lie.'

He was a little bald fellow with rimless glasses and he sat beside me on the bench outside the village post office where I was catching the afternoon edge of the April sun and reading an article called 'The Statistical Argument For ESP' in the Scientific Quarterly.

I had seen him glance at the title over my shoulder.

He was a little fellow – Cranston was his name – and he had been in the village since as long as I could remember. He was born up on Burley Creek in a log cabin but lived now with a widowed sister whose name was Berstauble and whose husband had been a sea captain. The captain had built one of those big towered and shingle-sided houses that looked down from the ridge onto the village and the sheltered waters of the Sound beyond. It was a weathered gray house half hidden by tall firs and hemlocks and it imparted an air of mystery to its occupants.

The immediate mystery to me was why Cranston had come down to the post office. They had a hired hand to run such errands. You seldom saw any of the family down in the village, although Cranston was sociable enough when you met him at the Grange hall and could be depended on for good conversation or a game of checkers.

Cranston stood about five feet four and weighed, I guess, about a hundred and fifty – so you can see he wasn't skinny. His clothing, winter or summer, was a visored painter's cap, a pair of bib overalls and a dark brown shirt of the kind the loggers wore – though I don't think he was ever a logger or, for that matter, ever did heavy labor of any kind.

'Something special bring you down to the post office?'

I asked in the direct and prying village manner. 'Don't see you down here very much.'

'I was . . . hoping to see someone,' he said. He nodded toward the Scientific Quarterly in my lap. 'Didn't know you were interested in extrasensory perception.'

There was no preventing it, I saw. I'm one of those people who attract confidences – even when we don't want confidences – and it was obvious Cranston had a 'story.' I tried once more to head him off, though, because I was in one of those moods writers get – where we'd just as soon bite off heads as look at them.

'I think ESP is a damned racket,' I said. 'And it's disgusting to see them twist logic trying to devise mathematical proofs for . . .'

'Well, I wouldn't be too sure if I were you,' he said. 'I could tell you a thing or two and that's no lie.'

'You read minds,' I said.

'Read's the wrong word,' he said. 'And it isn't minds . . .' Here, he stared once up the road that branches above the post office before looking back at me. 'It's mind.'

'You read a mind,' I said.

'I can see you don't believe,' he said. 'I'm going to tell you anyway. Never told an outsider before . . . but you're not really an outsider, your folks being who they are, and since you're a writer you may make something of this.'

I sighed and closed the Quarterly.

'I'd just moved up from the creek to live with my sister,' Cranston said. 'I was seventeen. She'd been married, let's see, about three years then, but her husband – the captain – was away at sea. To Hong Kong if I remember rightly. Her father-in-law, old Mr Jerusalem Berstauble, was living then. Had the downstairs bedroom that opens on the back porch. Deaf as a diver he was, for sure, and couldn't get out of his wheelchair without you helped him. Which was why they sent for me to come up from the creek. He was a living heller, old Mr Jerusalem, if you remember. But then you never knew him, I guess.'

(This was the sliding reference to my borderline status

that no villager seemed able to avoid when discussing 'olden times' with me – though they all accepted me because my grandparents were villagers and everyone in the valley knew I had 'come home' to recover from my wound in the war.)

'Old Mr Jerusalem dearly loved his game of cribbage in the evening,' Cranston said. 'This one evening I'm telling you about he and my sister were playing their game in the study. They didn't talk much because of his deafness and all we could hear through the open door of the study was the slap of the cards and my sister kind of muttering as she pegged each hand.

'We'd turned off the living room lights, but there was a fire in the fireplace and there was light from the study. I was sitting in the living room with Olna, the Norwegian girl who helped my sister then. She married Gus Bills a couple years later, the one killed when the donkey engine blew up at Indian Camp. Olna and I'd been playing a Norwegian card game they call *reap* which is something like whist, but we got tired of it and were just sitting there across the fireplace from each other halfway listening to the cards slapping down the way they did in the study.'

Cranston pushed back his visored painter's cap and glanced toward the green waters of the Sound where a tug was nursing a boom of logs out from the tidal basin.

'Oh, she was pretty then, Olna was,' he said presently. 'Her hair was like silvered gold. And her skin – it was like you could look right into it.'

'You were sweet on her,' I said.

'Daft is the word,' he said. 'And she didn't mind me one bit, either . . . at first there.'

Again, he fell silent. He tugged once at his cap visor. Presently, he said: 'I was trying to remember if it was my idea or hers. It was mine. Olna had the deck of cards still in her hands. And I said to her, "Olna, you shuffle the deck. Don't let me see the cards." Yes, that's how it was. I said for her to shuffle the deck and take one card at a time off the top and see if I could guess what it was.

'There was a lot of talk going around just then about

this fellow at Duke University, this doctor, I forget his name, who had these cards people guessed. I think that's what put the notion in my mind.'

Cranston fell silent a moment and I swear he looked younger for an instant – especially around the eyes.

'So you shuffled the cards,' I said, interested in spite of myself. 'What then?'

'Eh? Oh . . . she said: "Yah, see if you can guess diss vun." She had a thick accent, Olna. Would've thought she'd been born in the old country instead of over by Port Orchard. Well, she took that first card and looked at it. Lord, how pretty she was bending to catch the light from the study door. And you know, I knew the instant she saw it what it was – the jack of clubs. It was as though I saw it in my mind somewhere . . . not exactly seeing, but I knew. So I just blurted out what it was.'

'You got one right out of fifty-two . . . not bad,' I said.

'We went right through the deck and I named every card for her,' Cranston said. 'As she turned them up – every card; not one mistake.'

I didn't believe him, of course. These stories are a dime a dozen in the study of ESP, so I'm told. None of them pan out. But I *was* curious why he was telling this story. Was it the old village bachelor, the nobody, the man existing on a sister's charity trying to appear important?

'So you named every card for her,' I said. 'You ever figure the odds against that?'

'I had a professor over at the State College do it for me once,' Cranston said. 'I forget how much it was. He said it was impossible such a thing was chance.'

'Impossible,' I agreed not trying to disguise my disbelief. 'What did Olna think of this?'

'She thought it was a trick – parlor magic, you know.'

'She was wearing glasses and you saw the cards reflected in them, isn't that it?' I asked.

'She doesn't wear glasses to this day,' Cranston said.

'Then you saw them reflected in her eyes,' I said.

'She was sitting in shadows about ten feet away,' he

said. 'She only had the light from the study door to see the cards. She had to hold them toward the firelight from the fireplace for me to see them. No, it wasn't anything like that. Besides, I had my eyes closed some of the time. I just kind of saw those cards . . . this place in my mind that I found. I didn't have to hesitate or guess. I *knew* every time.'

'Well, that's very interesting,' I said, and I opened the Scientific Quarterly. 'Perhaps you should be back at Duke helping Dr Rhine.'

'You can bet I was excited,' he said, ignoring my attempt to end the conversation. 'This famous doctor had said humans could do this thing, and here I was proving it.'

'Yes,' I said. 'Perhaps you should write Dr Rhine and tell him.'

'I told Olna to shuffle the cards and we'd try it again,' Cranston said, his voice beginning to sound slightly desperate. 'She didn't seem too eager, but she did it. I did notice her hands were trembling.'

'You frightened the poor child with your parlor magic,' I said.

He sighed and sat there in silence for a moment staring at the waters of the Sound. The tug was chugging off with its boom of logs. I found myself suddenly feeling very sorry for this pitiful litle man. He had never been more than fifty miles from the village, I do believe. He lived a life bounded by that old house on the ridge, the weekly card games at the Grange and an occasional trip to the store for groceries. I don't even believe they had television. His sister was reputed to be a real old-fashioned harridan on the subject.

'Did you name all the cards again?' I asked, trying to sound interested.

'Without one mistake,' he said. 'I had that place in my mind firmly located by then. I could find my way to it every time.'

'And Olna wanted to know how you were doing it,' I said.

He swallowed. 'No. I think she . . . *felt* how I was doing it. We hadn't gone through more'n fifteen cards that second time when she threw the deck onto the floor. She sat there shivering and staring at me. Suddenly, she called me some names – I never did rightly hear it straights – and she leaped up and ran out of the house. It happened so fast! She was out the back door before I was on my feet. I ran out after her but she was gone. We found out later she hitched a ride on the bread truck and went straight home to Port Orchard. She never came back.'

'That's too bad,' I said. 'The one person whose mind you could read and she ran out on you.'

'She never came back,' he said, and I swear his voice had tears in it. 'Everyone thought . . . you know, that I'd made improper advances. My sister was pretty mad. Olna's brother came for her things the next day. He threatened to *whoomp* me if I ever set foot on . . .'

Cranston broke off, turning to stare up the gravel road that comes into the village from the hill farms to the west. A tall woman in a green dress that ended half way between knees and ankles had just turned the corner by the burned-out stump and was making for the post office. She walked with her head down so you could see part of the top of her head where the yellow hair was braided and wound tight like a crown. She was a big woman with a good figure and a healthy swing to her stride.

'I heard her brother was sick,' Cranston said.

I glanced at Cranston and the look on his face – sad and distant – answered my unspoken question.

'That's Olna,' I said. I began to feel excitement. I didn't believe his fool story, still . . .

'She doesn't come down here very often,' Cranston said. 'But with her brother sick, I'd hoped . . .'

She turned off onto the post office path and the corner of the building hid her from us. We heard the door open on the other side and a low mumble of conversation in the building. Presently, the door opened once more and the woman came around the corner, taking the path that passed in front of us toward the store down by the highway. She still had her head bent, but now she was reading a letter.

As she passed in front of us no more than six feet away, Cranston said: 'Olna?'

Her head whipped around and she stopped with one foot ahead of the other. I swear I've never seen more terror in a person's face. She just stared frozen at Cranston.

'I'm sorry about your sister's boy,' Cranston said, and then added: 'If I were you, I'd suggest she take the boy to one of those specialists in Minneapolis. They do wonders with plastic surgery nowadays and ...'

'You!' she screamed. Her right hand came up with the index and little fingers pointed at Cranston in a warding-off-evil sign that I'd thought died out in the middle ages. 'You stay out of my head ... you ... you *cottys!*'

Her words broke the spell. She picked up her skirts and fled down the path toward the highway. The last we saw of her was a running figure that sped around the corner by the garage.

I tried to find something to say, but nothing came. Cottys, that was the Danuan Pan who seduced virgins by capturing their minds, but I'd never realized that the Norse carried that legend around.

'Her sister just wrote her in that letter,' Cranston said, 'that the youngest boy was badly scalded by a kettle tipped off the stove. Just happened day before yesterday. That's an airmail letter. Don't get many of them here.'

'Are you trying to tell me you read that letter through her eyes?' I demanded.

'I never lost that place I found,' he said. 'Lord knows I tried to lose it often enough. Especially after she married Gus Bills.'

Excitement boiled in me. The possibilities ...

'Look,' I said. 'I'll write to Duke University myself. We can ...'

'Don't you dare!' he snapped. 'It's bad enough every man in the valley knows this about us. Oh, I know they mostly don't believe ... but the chance ...' He shook his head. 'I'll not stand in her way if she finds a suitable man to . . .'

'But, man,' I said. 'If you . . .'

'You believe me now, don't you?' he said, and his voice had a sly twist I didn't like.

'Well,' I said, 'I'd like to see this examined by people who . . .'

'Make it a sideshow,' he said. 'Stories in the Sunday papers. Whole world'd know.'

'But if . . .'

'She won't have me!' he barked. 'Don't you understand? She'll never lose me, but she won't have me. Even when she went on the train back to Minneapolis . . . the week after she ran out of our house . . .'

His voice trailed off.

'But think of what this could mean to . . .'

'There's the only woman I ever loved,' Cranston said. 'Only woman I ever could've married . . . she thinks I'm the devil himself!' He turned and glared at me. 'You think I want to expose *that?* I'd reach into my head with a bailing hook and tear that place out of my mind first!'

And with that he bounced to his feet and took off up the path that led toward the road to the ridge.

OPERATION SYNDROME

Honolulu is quiet, the dead buried, the rubble of buildings cleared away. A salvage barge rocks in the Pacific swell off Diamond Head. Divers follow a bubble trail down into the green water of the wreck of the Stateside skytrain. The Scramble Syndrome did this. Ashore, in converted barracks, psychologists work fruitlessly in the aftermath of insanity. This is where the Scramble Syndrome started: one minute the city was peaceful; a clock tick later the city was mad.

In forty days – nine cities infected.

The twentieth century's Black Plague.

SEATTLE

First a ringing in the ears, fluting up to a whistle. The whistle became the warning blast of a nightmare train roaring clackety-clack, clackety-clack across his dream.

A psychoanalyst might have enjoyed the dream as a clinical study. This psychoanalyst was not studying the dream; he was having it. He clutched the sheet around his neck, twisted silently on the bed, drawing his knees under his chin.

The train whistle modulated into the contralto of an expensive chanteuse singing 'Insane Crazy Blues.' The dream carried vibrations of fear and wildness.

'A million dollars don't mean a thing—'

Hoarse voice riding over clarion brass, bumping of drums, clarinet squealing like an angry horse.

A dark-skinned singer with electric blue eyes and dressed in black stepped away from a red backdrop. She opened her arms to an unseen audience. The singer, the backdrop lurched into motion, revolving faster and faster and faster until it merged into a pinpoint of red light. The red light dilated to the bell mouth of a trumpet sustaining a minor note.

The music shrilled; it was a knife cutting his brain.

Dr Eric Ladde awoke. He breathed rapidly; he oozed perspiration. Still he heard the singer, the music.

I'm dreaming that I'm awake, he thought.

He peeled off the top sheet, slipped his feet out, put them on the warm floor. Presently, he stood up, walked to the window, looked down on the moontrail shimmering across Lake Washington. He touched the sound switch beside the window and now he could hear the night – crickets, spring peepers at the lakeshore, the far hum of a skytrain.

The singing remained.

He swayed, gripped at the windowsill.

Scramble Syndrome—

He turned, examined the bedside newstape: no mention of Seattle. Perhaps he was safe – illness. But the music inside his head was no illness.

He made a desperate clutch for self-control, shook his head, banged his ear with the palm of his hand. The singing persisted. He looked to the bedside clock – 1:05am, Friday, May 14, 1999.

Inside his head the music stopped. But now – Applause! A roar of clapping, cries, stamping of feet. Eric rubbed his head.

I'm not insane . . . I'm not insane—

He slipped into his dressing gown, went into the kitchen cubicle of his bachelor residence. He drank water, yawned, held his breath – anything to drive away the noise, now a chicken-haggle of talking, clinking, slithering of feet.

He made himself a highball, splashed the drink at the back of his throat. The sounds inside his head turned off. Eric looked at the empty glass in his hand, shook his head.

A new specific for insanity – alcohol! He smiled wryly. *And every day I tell my patients that drinking is no solution.* He tasted a bitter thought: *Maybe I should have joined that therapy team, not stayed here trying to create a machine to cure the insane. If only they hadn't laughed at me—*

He moved a fibreboard box to make room beside the

sink, put down his glass. A notebook protruded from the
box, sitting atop a mound of electronic parts. He picked
up the notebook, stared at his own familiar block printing
on the cover: *Amanti Teleprobe – Test Book IX·*

They laughed at the old doctor, too, he thought. *Laughed
him right into an asylum. Maybe that's where I'm headed
– along with everyone else in the world.*

He opened the notebook, traced his finger along the
diagram of his latest experimental circuit. The teleprobe in
his basement laboratory still carried the wiring, partially
dismantled.

What was wrong with it?

He closed the notebook, tossed it back into the box. His
thoughts hunted through the theories stored in his mind,
the knowledge saved from a thousand failures. Fatigue and
despondency pulled at him. Yet, he knew that the things
Freud, Jung, Adler and all the others had sought in dreams
and mannerisms hovered just beyond his awareness in an
electronic tracer circuit.

He wandered back into his study-bedroom, crawled into
the bed. He practiced yoga breathing until sleep washed
over him. The singer, the train, the whistle did not return.

Morning lighted the bedroom. He awoke, trailing frag-
ments of his nightmare into consciousness, aware that his
appointment book was blank until ten o'clock. The bedside
newstape offered a long selection of stories, most headed
'Scramble Syndrome.' He punched code letters for eight
items, flipped the machine to audio and listened to the
news while dressing.

Memory of his nightmare nagged at him. He wondered,
'How many people awake in the night, asking themselves,
"Is it my turn now?" '

He selected a mauve cape, drew it over his white coveralls. Retrieving the notebook from the box in the kitchen,
he stepped out into the chill spring morning. He turned up
the temperature adjustment of his coveralls. The unitube
whisked him to the Elliott Bay waterfront. He ate at a sea-

food restaurant, the teleprobe notebook open beside his
plate. After breakfast, he found an empty bench outside
facing the bay, sat down, opened the notebook. He found
himself reluctant to study the diagrams, stared out at the
bay.

Mists curled from the gray water, obscuring the opposite shore. Somewhere in the drift a purse seiner sounded
its hooter. Echoes bounced off the buildings behind him.
Early workers hurried past, voices stilled: thin look of
faces, hunted glances – the uniform of fear. Coldness from
the bench seeped through his clothing. He shivered, drew
a deep breath of the salt air. The breeze off the bay carried
essence of seaweed, harmonic on the dominant bitter musk
of a city's effluvia. Seagulls haggled over a morsel in the
tide rip. The papers on his lap fluttered. He held them
down with one hand, watching the people.

I'm procrastinating, he thought. *It's a luxury my pro-
fession can ill afford nowadays.*

A woman in a red fur cape approached, her sandals
tapping a swift rhythm on the concrete. Her cape billowed
behind in a puff of breeze.

He looked up to her face framed in dark hair. Every
muscle in his body locked. She was the woman of his
nightmare down to the minutest detail! His eyes followed
her. She saw him staring, looked away, walked past.

Eric fumbled his papers together, closed the notebook
and ran after her. He caught up, matched his steps to hers,
still staring, unthinking. She looked at him, flushed, looked
away.

'Go away or I'll call a cop!'

'Please, I have to talk to you.'

'I said go away.' She increased her pace; he matched it.

'Please forgive me, but I dreamed about you last night.
You see—'

She stared straight ahead.

'I've been told *that* one before! Go away!'

'But you don't understand.'

She stopped, turned and faced him, shaking with anger.

'But I *do* understand! You saw my show last night! You've dreamed about me!' She wagged her head. 'Miss Lanai, I *must* get to know you!'

Eric shook his head. 'But I've never even heard of you or seen you before.'

'Well! I'm not accustomed to being insulted either!' She whirled, walked away briskly, the red cape flowing out behind her. Again he caught up with her.

'Please—'

'I'll scream!'

'I'm a psychoanalyst.'

She hesitated, slowed, stopped. A puzzled expression flowed over her face. 'Well, that's a new approach.'

He took advantage of her interest. 'I really did dream about you. It was most disturbing. I couldn't shut it off.'

Something in his voice, his manner— She laughed, 'A real dream was bound to show up some day.'

'I'm Dr Eric Ladde.'

She glanced at the caduceus over his breast pocket. 'I'm Colleen Lanai; I sing.'

He winced. 'I know.'

'I thought you'd never heard of me.'

'You sang in my dream.'

'Oh.' A pause. 'Are you really a psychoanalyst?'

He slipped a card from his breast pocket; handed it to her. She looked at it.

'What does "Teleprobe Diagnosis" mean?'

'That's an instrument I use.'

She returned the card, linked an arm through his, set an easy, strolling pace. 'All right, doctor. You tell me about your dream and I'll tell you about my headaches. Fair exchange?' She peered up at him from under thick eyelashes.

'Do you have headaches?'

'Terrible headaches.' She shook her head.

Eric looked down at her. Some of the nightmare unreality returned. He thought, 'What am I doing here? One doesn't dream about a strange face and then meet her in the flesh the next day. The next thing I know the whole world of my unconscious will come alive.'

'Could it be this Syndrome thing?' she asked. 'Ever since we were in Los Angeles I've—' She chewed at her lip.

He stared at her. 'You were in Los Angeles?'

'We got out just a few hours before that . . . before—' She shuddered. 'Doctor, what's it like to be crazy?'

He hesitated. 'It's no different from being sane – for the person involved.' He looked out at the mist lifting from the bay. 'The Syndrome appears similar to other forms of insanity. It's as though something pushed people over their lunacy thresholds. It's strange; there's a rather well defined radius of about sixty miles which it saturated. Atlanta and Los Angeles, for instance, and Lawton, had quite sharp lines of demarcation: people on one side of a street got it; people on the other side didn't. We suspect there's a contamination period during which—' He paused, looked down at her, smiled. 'And all you asked was a simple question. This is my lecture personality. I wouldn't worry too much about those headaches; probably diet, change of climate, maybe your eyes. Why don't you get a complete physical?'

She shook her head. 'I've had six physicals since we left Karachi: same thing – four new diets.' She shrugged. 'Still I have headaches.'

Eric jerked to a stop, exhaled slowly. 'You were in Karachi, too?'

'Why, yes; that was the third place we hit after Honolulu.'

He leaned toward her. 'And Honolulu?'

She frowned. 'What is this, a cross-examination?' She waited. 'Well—'

He swallowed, thought, *How can one person have been in these cities the Syndrome hit and be so casual about it?*

She tapped a foot. 'Cat got your tongue?'

He thought, *She's so flippant about it.*

He ticked off the towns on his fingers. 'You were in Los

Angeles, Honolulu, Karachi; you've hit the high spots of Syndrome contamination and—'

An animal cry, sharp, exclamatory, burst from her. 'It got all of those places?'

He thought, *How could anyone be alive and not know exactly where the Syndrome has been?*

He asked, 'Didn't you know?'

She shook her head, a numb motion, eyes wide, staring. 'But Pete said—' She stopped. 'I've been so busy learning new numbers. We're reviving the old time hot jazz.'

'How could you miss it? TV is full of it, the newstapes, the transgraphs.'

She shrugged. 'I've just been so busy. And I don't like to think about such things. Pete said—' She shook her head. 'You know, this is the first time I've been out alone for a walk in over a month. Pete was asleep and—' Her expression softened. 'That Pete; he must have not wanted me to worry.'

'If you say so, but—' He stopped. 'Who's Pete?'

'Haven't you heard of Pete Serantis and the musikron?'

'What's a musikron?'

She shook back a curl of dark hair. 'Have your little joke, doctor.'

'No, seriously. What's a musikron?'

She frowned. 'You *really* don't know what the musikron is?'

He shook his head.

She chuckled, a throaty sound, controlled. 'Doctor, you talk about *my* not knowing about Karachi and Honolulu. Where have you been hiding your head? *Variety* has us at the top of the heap.'

He thought, 'She's serious!'

A little stiffly, he said, 'Well, I've been quite busy with a research problem of my own. It deals with the Syndrome.'

'Oh.' She turned, looked at the gray waters of the bay, turned back. She twisted her hands together. 'Are you sure about Honolulu?'

'Is your family there?'

She shook her head. 'I have no family. Just friends.' She looked up at him, eyes shining. 'Did it get . . . everybody?'

He nodded, thought: *She needs something to distract her attention.*

He said, 'Miss Lanai, could I ask you a favor?' He plunged ahead, not waiting for an answer. 'You've been three places where the Syndrome hit. Maybe there's a clue in your patterns. Would you consent to undergoing a series of tests at my lab? They wouldn't take long.'

'I couldn't possibly; I have a show to do tonight. I just sneaked out for a few minutes by myself. I'm at the Gweduc Room. Pete may wake up and—' She focused on his pleading expression. 'I'm sorry, doctor. Maybe some other time. You wouldn't find anything important from me anyway.'

He shrugged, hesitated. 'But I haven't told you about my dream.'

'You tempt me, doctor. I've heard a lot of phony dream reports. I'd appreciate the McCoy for just once. Why don't you walk me back to the Gweduc Room? It's only a couple of blocks.'

'Okay.'

She took his arm.

'Half a loaf—'

He was a thin man with a twisted leg, a pinched, hating face. A cane rested against his knee. Around him wove a spiderweb maze of wires – musikron. On his head, a dome-shaped hood. A spy, unsuspected, he looked out through a woman's eyes at a man who had identified himself as Dr Eric Ladde. The thin man sneered, heard through the woman's ears: 'Half a loaf—'

On the bayside walk, Eric and Colleen matched steps.

'You never did tell me what a musikron is.'

Her laughter caused a passing couple to turn and stare.

'OK. But I still don't understand. We've been on TV for a month.'

He thought, *She thinks I'm a fuddy; probably am!*

He said, 'I don't subscribe to the entertainment circuits. I'm just on the science and news networks.'

She shrugged. 'Well, the musikron is something like a recording and playback machine; only the operator mixes in any new sounds he wants. He wears a little metal bowl on his head and just thinks about the sounds – the musikron plays them.' She stole a quick glance at him, looked ahead. 'Everyone says it's a fake; it really isn't.'

Eric stopped, pulled her to a halt. 'That's fantastic. Why—' He paused, chuckled. 'You know, you happen to be talking to one of the few experts in the world on this sort of thing. I have an encephalo-recorder in my basement lab that's the last word in teleprobes . . . that's what you're trying to describe.' He smiled. 'The psychiatrists of this town may think I'm a young upstart, but they send me their tough diagnostic cases.' He looked down at her. 'So let's just admit your Pete's machine is artistic showmanship, shall we?'

'But it isn't just showmanship. I've heard the records before they go into the machine and when they come out of it.'

Eric chuckled.

She frowned. 'O, you're so supercilious.'

Eric put a hand on her arm. 'Please don't be angry. It's just that I know this field. You don't want to admit that Pete has fooled you along with all the others.'

She spoke in a slow, controlled cadence: 'Look . . . doctor . . . Pete . . . was . . . one . . . of . . . the . . . inventors . . . of . . . the . . . musikron . . . Pete . . . and . . . old . . . Dr . . . Amanti.' She squinted her eyes, looking up at him. 'You may be a big wheel in this business, but I know what I've heard.'

'You said Pete worked on this musikron with a doctor. What did you say that doctor's name was?'

'Oh, Dr Carlos Amanti. His name's on a little plate inside the musikron.'

Eric shook his head. 'Impossible. Dr Carlos Amanti is in an asylum.'

She nodded. 'That's right; Wailiku Hospital for the Insane. That's where they worked on it.'

Eric's expression was cautious, hesitant. 'And you say when Pete thinks about the sounds, the machine produces them?'

'Certainly.'

'Strange I'd never heard about this musikron before.'

'Doctor, there are a lot of things you've never heard about.'

He wet his lips with his tongue. 'Maybe you're right.' He took her arm, set a rapid pace down the walkway. 'I want to see this musikron.'

In Lawton, Oklahoma, long rows of prefabricated barracks swelter on a sunbaked flat. In each barracks building, little cubicles; in each cubicle, a hospital bed; on each hospital bed, a human being. Barracks XRO-29: a psychiatrist walks down the hall, behind him an orderly pushing a cart. On the cart, hypodermic needles, syringes, antiseptics, sedatives, test tubes. The psychiatrist shakes his head.

'Baily, they certainly nailed this thing when they called it the Scramble Syndrome. Stick an egg-beater into every psychosis a person could have, mix 'em up, turn 'em all on.'

The orderly grunts, stares at the psychiatrist.

The psychiatrist looks back. 'And we're not making any progress on this thing. It's like bailing out the ocean with a sieve.'

Down the hallway a man screams. Their footsteps quicken.

The Gweduc Room's elevator dome arose ahead of Eric and Colleen, a half-melon inverted on the walkway. At the top of the dome a blue and red script-ring circled slowly, spelling out, 'Colleen Lanai with Pete Serantis and the Musikron.'

On the walkway before the dome a thin man, using a cane to compensate for a limp, paced back and forth. He looked up as Eric and Colleen approached.

'Pete,' she said.

The man limped toward them, his cane staccato on the paving.

'Pete, this is Dr Ladde. He's heard about Dr Amanti and he wants to—'

Pete ignored Eric, stared fiercely at Colleen. 'Don't you know we have a show tonight? Where have you been?'

'But, it's only a little after nine; I don't—'

Eric interrupted. 'I was a student of Dr Amanti's. I'm interested in your musikron. You see, I've been carrying on Dr Amanti's researches and—'

The thin man barked, 'No time!' He took Colleen's arm, pulled her toward the dome.

'Pete, please! What's come over you?' She held back.

Pete stopped, put his face close to hers. 'Do you like this business?'

She nodded mutely, eyes wide.

'Then let's get to work!'

She looked back at Eric, shrugged her shoulders. 'I'm sorry.'

Pete pulled her into the dome.

Eric stared after them. He thought, 'He's a decided compulsive type . . . very unstable. May not be as immune to the Syndrome as she apparently is.' He frowned, looked at his wrist watch, remembered his ten o'clock appointment. 'Damn!' He turned, almost collided with a young man in busboy's coveralls.

The young man puffed nervously at a cigarette, jerked it out of his mouth, leered. 'Better find yourself another gal, Doc. That one's taken.'

Eric looked into the young-old eyes, stared them down. 'You work in there?'

The young man replaced the cigarette between thin lips, spoke around a puff of blue smoke. 'Yeah.'

'When does it open?'

The young man pulled the cigarette from his mouth, flipped it over Eric's shoulder into the bay. 'We're open now for breakfast. Floor show doesn't start until seven tonight.'

'Is Miss Lanai in the floor show?'

The busboy looked up at the script-ring over the dome, smiled knowingly. 'Doc, she *is* the floor show!'

Again Eric looked at his wrist watch, thought, *I'm coming back here tonight*. He turned toward the nearest unitube. 'Thanks,' he said.

'You better get reservations if you're coming back to-night,' said the busboy.

Eric stopped, looked back. He reached into his pocket, found a twenty-buck piece, flipped it to the busboy. The thin young man caught the coin out of the air, looked at it, said, 'Thank *you*. What name, Doc?'

'Dr Eric Ladde.'

The busboy pocketed the coin. 'Righto, Doc. Floorside. I come on again at six. I'll attend to you personally.'

Eric turned back to the unitube entrance again and left immediately.

Under the smog-filtered Los Angeles sun, a brown-dry city.

Mobile Laboratory 31 ground to a stop before Our Lady of Mercy Hospital, churning up a swirl of dried palm fronds in the gutter. The overworked turbo-motor sighed to a stop, grating. The Japanese psychologist emerged on one side, the Swedish doctor on the other. Their shoulders sagged.

The psychologist asked, 'Ole, how long since you've had a good night's sleep?'

The doctor shook his head. 'I can't remember, Yoshi; not since I left Frisco, I guess.'

From the caged rear of the truck, wild, high-pitched laughter, a sigh, laughter.

The doctor stumbled on the steps to the hospital sidewalk. He stopped, turned. 'Yoshi—'

'Sure, Ole. I'll get some fresh orderlies to take care of this one.' To himself he added, 'If there are any fresh orderlies.'

Inside the hospital, cool air pressed down the hallway. The Swedish doctor stopped a man with a clipboard. 'What's the latest count?'

The man scratched his forehead with a corner of the clipboard. 'Two and a half million last I heard, doctor. They haven't found a sane one yet.'

The Gweduc Room pointed a plastine finger under Elliott Bay. Unseen by the patrons, a cage compressed a high density of sea life over the transparent ceiling. Illumabeams traversed the water, treating the watchers to visions of a yellow salmon, a mauve perch, a pink octopus, a blue jellyfish. At one end of the room, synthetic mother-of-pearl had been formed into a giant open gweduc shell – the stage. Colored spotlights splashed the backdrop with ribbons of flame, blue shadows.

Eric went down the elevator, emerged in an atmosphere disturbingly reminiscent of his nightmare. All it lacked was the singer. A waiter led him, threading a way through the dim haze of perfumed cigarette smoke, between tables ringed by men in formal black, women in gold lamé, luminous synthetics. An aquamarine glow shimmered from the small round table tops – the only lights in the Gweduc Room other than spotlights on the stage and illumabeams in the dark water overhead. A susurration of many voices hung on the air. Aromas of alcohol, tobacco, perfumes, exotic seafoods layered the room, mingled with a perspirant undertone.

The table nestled in the second row, crowded on all sides. The waiter extricated a chair; Eric sat down.

'Something to drink, sir?'

'Bombay Ale.'

The waiter turned, merged into the gloom.

Eric tried to move his chair into a comfortable position, found it was wedged immovably between two chairs behind him. A figure materialized out of the gloom across from him; he recognized the busboy.

'Best I could get you, Doc.'

'This is excellent.' Eric smiled, fished a twenty-buck piece from his pocket, pressed it into the other's hand.

'Anything I can do for you Doc?'

'Would you tell Miss Lanai I'm here?'

'I'll try, Doc; but that Pete character has been watching her like a piece of prize property all afternoon. Not that I wouldn't do the same thing myself, you understand.'

White teeth flashed in the smoky-layered shadows. The busboy turned, weaved his way back through the tables. The murmuring undercurrent of voices in the room damped out. Eric turned toward the stage. A portly man in ebony and chalk-striped coveralls bent over the microphone.

'Here's what you've been waiting for,' he said. He gestured with his left hand. Spotlights erased a shadow, revealing Colleen Lanai, her hands clasped in front of her. An old-fashioned gown of electric blue to match her eyes sheathed the full curves.

'Colleen Lanai!'

Applause washed over the room, subsided. The portly man gestured with his right hand. Other spotlights flared, revealing Pete Serantis in black coveralls, leaning on his cane.

'Pete Serantis and—'

He waited for a lesser frenzy of clapping to subside.

'. . . The Musikron!'

A terminal spotlight illuminated a large metallic box behind Pete. The thin man limped around the box, ducked, and disappeared inside. Colleen took the microphone from the announcer, who bowed and stepped off the stage.

Eric became aware of a pressing mood of urgency in the room. He thought, 'For a brief instant we forget our fears, forget the Syndrome, everything except the music and this instant.'

Colleen held the microphone intimately close to her mouth.

'We have some more real oldies for you tonight,' she said. An electric pressure of personality pulsed out from her. 'Two of these songs we've never presented before. First, a trio – "Terrible Blues" with the musikron giving you a basic recording by Clarence Williams and the Red Onion Jazz Babies, Pete Serantis adding an entirely new effect; next, "Wild Man Blues" and the trumpet is pure Louis Armstrong; last, "Them's Graveyard Words," an old Bessie Smith special.' She bowed almost imperceptibly.

Music appeared in the room, not definable as to direction. It filled the senses. Colleen began to sing, seemingly without effort. She played her voice like a horn, soaring with the music, ebbing with it, caressing the air with it.

Eric stared, frozen, with all the rest of the audience.

She finished the first song. The noise of applause deafened him. He felt pain in his hands, looked down to find himself beating his palms together. He stopped, shook his head, took four deep breaths. Colleen picked up the thread of a new melody. Eric narrowed his eyes, staring at the stage. Impulsively, he put his hands to his ears and felt panic swell as the music remained undiminished. He closed his eyes, caught his breath as he continued to see Colleen, blurred at first, shifting, then in a steady image from a place nearer and to the left.

A wavering threnody of emotions accompanied the vision. Eric put his hands before his eyes. The image remained. He opened his eyes. The image again blurred, shifted to normal. He searched to one side of Colleen for the position from which he had been seeing her. He decided it could only be from inside the musikron and at the instant of decision discerned the outline of a mirror panel in the face of the metallic box.

'Through a one-way glass,' he thought. 'Through Pete's eyes.'

He sat, thinking, while Colleen finished her third number. Pete emerged from the musikron to share the applause. Colleen blew a kiss to the audience.

'We'll be back in a little while.'

She stepped down from the stage, followed by Pete; darkness absorbed them. Waiters moved along the tables. A drink was placed on Eric's table. He put money in the tray. A blue shadow appeared across from him, slipped into the chair.

'Tommy told me you were here . . . the busboy.' She leaned across the table. 'You mustn't let Pete see you. He's in a rage, a real pet. I've never seen anybody that angry.'

Eric leaned toward her, caught a delicate exhalation of sandalwood perfume. It dizzied him. 'I want to talk to you,' he said. 'Can you meet me after the show?'

'I guess I can trust you,' she said. She hesitated, smiling faintly. 'You're the professional type.' Another pause. 'And I think I need professional advice.' She slipped out of the chair, stood up. 'I have to get back before he suspects I didn't go to the powder room. I'll meet you near the freight elevator upstairs.'

She was gone.

A cold breeze off the bay tugged at Eric's cape, puffing it out behind him. He leaned against the concrete railing, drawing on a cigarette. The glowing coal flowed an orange wash across his face, flaring, dimming. The tide rip sniggled and babbled; waves lap-lap-lapped at the concrete beneath him. A multi-colored glow in the water to his left winked out as the illumabeams above the Gweduc Room were extinguished. He shivered. Footsteps approached from his left, passed behind him – a man, alone. A muffled whirring sound grew, stopped. Light footsteps ran toward him, stopped at the rail. He smelled her perfume.

'Thanks,' he said.

'I can't be long. He's suspicious. Tommy brought me up the freight elevator. He's waiting.'

'I'll be brief. I've been thinking. I'm going to talk about

travel. I'm going to tell you where you've been since you hooked up with Pete in Honolulu.' He turned, leaned sideways against the railing. 'You tried your show first in Santa Rosa, California, the sticks; then you went to Piquetberg, Karachi, Reykjavik, Portland, Hollandia, Lawton – finally, Los Angeles. Then you came here.'

'So you looked up our itinerary.'

He shook his head. 'No.' He hesitated. 'Pete's kept you pretty busy rehearsing, hasn't he?'

'This isn't easy work.'

'I'm not saying it is.' He turned back to the rail, flipped his cigarette into the darkness, heard it hiss in the water. 'How long have you known Pete?'

'A couple of months more or less. Why?'

He turned away. 'What kind of a fellow is he?'

She shrugged. 'He's a nice guy. He's asked me to marry him.'

Eric swallowed. 'Are you going to?'

She looked out to the dark bay. 'That's why I want your advice. I don't know . . . I just don't know. He put me where I am, right on top of the entertainment heap.' She turned back to Eric. 'And he really is an awfully nice guy . . . when you get under that bitterness.'

Eric breathed deeply, pressed against the concrete railing. 'May I tell you a story?'

'What about?'

'This morning you mentioned Dr Carlos Amanti, the inventor of the teleprobe. Did you know him?'

'No.'

'I was one of his students. When he had the breakdown it hit all of us pretty hard, but I was the only one who took up the teleprobe project. I've been working at it eight years.'

She stirred beside him. 'What is this teleprobe?'

'The science writers have poked fun at it; they call it the "mind reader." It's not. It's just a means of interpreting some of the unconscious impulses of the human brain. I suppose some day it may approach mind reading. Right now it's a rather primitive instrument, sometimes unpredictable. Amanti's intention was to communicate with the unconscious mind, using interpretation of encephalographic waves. The idea was to amplify them, maintain a discrete separation between types, and translate the type variations according to thought images.'

She chewed her lower lip. 'And you think the musikron would help make a better teleprobe, that it would help fight the Syndrome?'

'I think more than that.' He looked down at the paving.

'You're trying to tell me something without saying it,' she said. 'Is it about Pete?'

'Not exactly.'

'Why'd you give that long recitation of where we'd been? That wasn't just idle talk. What are you driving at?'

He looked at her speculatively, weighing her mood. 'Hasn't Pete told you about those places?'

She put a hand to her mouth, eyes wide, staring. She moaned. 'Not the Syndrome . . . not all of those places, too?'

'Yes.' It was a flat, final sound.

She shook her head. 'What are you trying to tell me?'

'That it could be the musikron causing all of this.'

'Oh, no!'

'I could be wrong. But look at how it appears. Amanti was a genius working near the fringe of insanity. He had a psychotic break. Then he helped Pete build a machine. It's possible that machine picks up the operator's brain wave patterns, transmits them as a scrambling impulse. The musikron *does* convert thought into a discernible energy – sound. Why isn't it just as possible that it funnels a disturbing impulse directly into the unconscious?' He wet his lips with his tongue. 'Did you know that I hear those sounds even with my hands over my ears, see you with my eyes covered. Remember my nightmare? My nervous system is responding to a subjective impulse.'

'Does it do the same thing to everybody?'

'Probably not. Unless a person was conditioned as I

have been by spending years in the aura of a similar machine, these impulses would be censored at the threshold of consciousness. They would be repressed as unbelievable.'

Her lips firmed. She shook her head. 'I don't see how all this scientific gobbledy-gook proves the musikron caused the Syndrome.'

'Maybe it doesn't. But it's the best possibility I've seen. That's why I'm going to ask a favor. Could you get me the circuit diagrams for the musikron? If I could see them I'd be able to tell you just what this thing does. Do you know if Pete has plans for it?'

'There's some kind of a thick notebook inside the musikron. I think that's what you mean.'

'Could you get it?'

'Maybe, but not tonight . . . and I wouldn't dare tell Pete.'

'Why not tonight?'

'Pete sleeps with the key to the musikron. He keeps it locked when it's not in use; so no one will get inside and get a shock. It has to be left on all the time because it takes so long to warm it up. Something about crystals or energy potential or some words like that.'

'Where's Pete staying?'

'There are quarters down there, special apartments.'

He turned away, breathed the damp salt air, turned back.

Colleen shivered. 'I know it's not the musikron. I . . . they—' She was crying.

He moved closer, put an arm around her shoulders, waiting. He felt her shiver. She leaned against him; the shivering subsided.

'I'll get those plans.' She moved her head restlessly. 'That'll prove it isn't the musikron.'

'Colleen . . .' He tightened his arm on her shoulders, feeling a warm urgency within him.

She moved closer. 'Yes.'

He bent his head. Her lips were warm and soft. She clung to him, pulled away, nestled in his arms.

'This isn't right,' she said.

Again he bent his head. She tipped her head up to meet him. It was a gentle kiss.

She pulled away slowly, turned her head toward the bay. 'It can't be like this,' she whispered. 'So quick – without warning.'

He put his face in her hair, inhaled. 'Like what?'

'Like you'd found your way home.'

He swallowed. 'My dear.'

Again their lips met. She pulled away, put a hand to his cheek. 'I have to go.'

'When will I see you?'

'Tomorrow. I'll tell Pete I have to do some shopping.'

'Where?'

'Do you have a laboratory?'

'At my home in Chalmers Place on the other side of the lake. It's in the directory.'

'I'll come as soon as I can get the diagrams.'

Again they kissed.

'I really have to go.'

He held her tightly.

'Really.' She pulled away. 'Good night' – she hesitated – 'Eric.' Shadows flowed in around her.

He heard the whirring of the elevator, leaned back against the concrete, drawing deep breaths to calm himself.

Deliberate footsteps, approached from his left. A handlight flashed in his face, the dull gleam of a night patrolman's brassard behind the light. The light moved to the caduceus at his breast.

'You're out late, doctor.'

The light returned to his face, winked off. Eric knew he had been photographed – as a matter of routine.

'Your lipstick's smudged,' the patrolman said. He walked away past the elevator dome.

Inside the silent musikron: a thin man, pinched face,

hating. Bitter thought: *Now wasn't that a sweet love scene!*
Pause. *The doctor wants something to read?* Wry smile.
I'll provide *it. He'll have something to occupy his mind*
after we've gone.

Before going to bed, Eric filed a transgraph to Mrs Bertz,
his secretary, telling her to cancel his appointments for the
next day. He snuggled up to the pillow, hugging it. Sleep
avoided him. He practiced yoga breathing. His senses
remained alert. He slipped out of bed, put on a robe and
sandals. He looked at the bedside clock – 2:05am, Saturday, May 15, 1999. He thought, *Just twenty-five hours ago*
– nightmare. Now . . . I don't know. He smiled. *Yes I do;*
I'm in love. I feel like a college kid.

He took a deep breath. *I'm in love.* He closed his eyes
and looked at a memory picture of Colleen. *Eric, if you*
only solve this Syndrome, the world is yours. The thoughts
skipped a beat. *I'm an incipient manic—*

Eric ruminated. *If Pete takes that musikron out of*
Seattle— What then?

He snapped a finger, went to the vidiphone, called an
all-night travel agency. A girl clerk finally agreed to look
up the booking dates he wanted – for a special fee. He
gave her his billing code, broke the connection and went
to the microfilm rack across from the foot of his bed. He
ran a finger down the title index, stopped at 'Implications
of Encephalographic Wave Forms, A Study of the Nine
Brain Pulses, by Dr Carlos Amanti.' He pushed the selector
opposite the tape, activated the screen above the rack and
returned to his bed, carrying the remote-control unit.

The first page flashed on the screen; room lights dimmed
automatically. He read:

'There is a scale of vibratory impulses spanning and
exceeding the human auditory range which consistently
produce emotional responses of fear in varying degrees.
Certain of these vibratory impulses – loosely grouped under the term *sounds* – test the extremes of human emotional
experience. One may say, within reason, that all emotion

is response to stimulation by harmonic movement, by oscillation.

'Many workers have linked emotions with characteristic encephalographic wave responses: Carter's work on Zeta waves and love; Reymann on Pi waves and abstract thinking; Poulson on the Theta Wave Index to degrees of sorrow, to name a few.

'It is the purpose of my work to trace these characteristic responses and point out what I believe to be an entirely new direction for interpretation of—'

Because of the late hour, Eric had expected drowsiness to overtake his reading, but his senses grew more alert as he read. The words had the familiarity of much re-reading, but they still held stimulation. He recalled a passage toward the end of the book, put the film on motor feed and scanned forward to the section he wanted. He slowed the tape, returned the controls to single-page advance; there it was:

'While working with severely disturbed patients in the teleprobe, I have found a charged emotional feeling in the atmosphere. Others, unfamiliar with my work, have reported this same experience. This suggests that the characteristic emanations of a disturbed mentality may produce sympathetic reactions upon those within the unshielded field of the teleprobe. Strangely, this disturbed sensation sometimes follows by minutes or even hours the period when the patient was under examination.

'I am hesitant to suggest a theory based upon this latter phenomenon. There is too much we do not know about the teleprobe – its latency period, for instance. However, it is possible that the combination of teleprobe and disturbed personality broadcasts a field with a depressant effect upon the unconscious functions of persons within that field. Be that as it may, this entire field of teleprobe and encephalographic wave research carries implications which—'

With a decisive gesture, Eric snapped off the projector, slipped out of bed and dressed. The bedside clock showed

3:28am, Saturday, May 15 1999. Never in his life had he felt more alert. He took the steps two at a time down to his basement lab, flipped on all the lights, wheeled out his teleprobe.

I'm on to something, he thought. *This Syndrome problem is too urgent for me to waste time sleeping.*

He stared at his teleprobe, an open framework of shelves, banks of tubes, maze of wiring, relaxing chair in the center with the metal hemisphere of the pickup directly above the chair. He thought, *The musikron is rigged for sound projection; that means a secondary resonance circuit of some kind.*

He pulled an unused tape recorder from a rack at the end of his bench, stripped the playback circuit from it. He took the recorder service manual, sketched in the changes he would need, pausing occasionally to figure circuit loads and balances on a slide rule. Presently, not too satisfied with his work, but anxious to get started, he brought out the parts he would need and began cutting and soldering. In two hours he had what he wanted.

Eric took cutter pliers, went to the teleprobe, snipped away the recorder circuit, pulled it out as a unit. He wheeled the teleprobe cage to the bench and, delicately feeling his way, checking circuit diagrams as he went, he wired in the playback circuit. From the monitor and audio sides, he took the main leads, fed them back into the first bank of the encephalographic pickup. He put a test power source on the completed circuit and began adding resistance units by eye to balance the impedance. It took more than an hour of testing and cutting, required several units of shielding.

He stepped back, stared at the machine. He thought, *It's going to oscillate all over the place. How does he balance this monster?*

Eric pulled at his chin, thinking. *Well, let's see what this hybrid does.*

The wall clock above his bench showed 6:45am. He took a deep breath, hooked an overload fuse into a relay power switch, closed the switch. A wire in the pickup circuit blazed to incandescence; the fuse kicked out. Eric opened the switch, picked up a test meter, and returned to the machine. The fault eluded him. He went back to the circuit diagrams.

'Perhaps too much power—' He recalled that his heavy duty rheostat was at a shop being repaired, considered bringing out the auxiliary generator he had used on one experiment. The generator was beneath a pile of boxes in a corner. He put the idea temporarily aside, turned back to the teleprobe.

'If I could just get a look at that musikron.'

He stared at the machine. 'A resonance circuit— What else?' He tried to imagine the interrelationship of the components, fitting himself into the machine.

'I'm missing it some place! There's some other thing and I have the feeling I already know it, that I've heard it. I've got to see the diagrams on that musikron.'

He turned away, went out of the lab and climbed the stairs to his kitchen. He took a coffee capsule from a package in the cupboard, put it beside the sink. The vidiphone chimed. It was the clerk from the travel bureau. Eric took down her report, thanked her, broke the connection. He did a series of subtractions.

'Twenty-eight hour time lag,' he thought. 'Every one of them. That's too much of a coincidence.'

He experienced a moment of vertigo, followed by weariness. 'I'd better get some rest. I'll come back to this thing when I'm more alert.'

He padded into the bedroom, sat down on the bed, kicked off his sandals and lay back, too tired to undress. Sleep eluded him. He opened his eyes, looked at the clock: 7:00am. He sighed, closed his eyes, sank into a somnolent state. A niggling worry gnawed at his consciousness. Again he opened his eyes, looked at the clock: 9:50am. *But I didn't feel the time pass*, he thought. *I must have slept*. He closed his eyes. His senses drifted into dizziness, the current in a stream, a ship on the current, wandering, hunting, whirling.

He thought, *I hope he didn't see me leave.*

His eyelids snapped open and, for a moment, he saw a unitube entrance on the ceiling above his head. He shook his head.

'That was a crazy thought. Where'd that come from?' he asked himself. 'I've been working too hard.'

He turned on his side, returned to the somnolent state, his eyes drooping closed. Instantly, he had the sensation of being in a maze of wires; an emotion of hate surged over him so strongly it brought panic because he couldn't explain it or direct it at anything. He gritted his teeth, shook his head, opened his eyes. The emotion disappeared, leaving him weak. He closed his eyes. Into his senses crept an almost overpowering aroma of gardenias, a vision of dawnlight through a shuttered window. His eyelids snapped open; he sat up in the bed, put his head in his hands.

Rhinencephalic stimulation, he thought. *Visual stimulation . . . auditory stimulation . . . nearly total sensorium response. It means something. But what does it mean?* He shook his head, looked at the clock: 10:10am.

Outside Karachi, Pakistan, a Hindu holy man squatted in the dust beside an ancient road. Past him paraded a caravan of International Red Cross trucks, moving selected cases of Syndrome madmen to the skytrain field on the Indus delta. Tomorrow the sick would be studied at a new clinic in Vienna. The truck motors whined and roared; the ground trembled. The holy man drew an ancient symbol with a finger in the dust. The wind of a passing truck stirred the pattern of Brahmaputra, twisting it. The holy man shook his head sadly.

Eric's front door announcer chimed as someone stepped onto the entrance mat. He clicked the scanner switch at his bedside, looked to the bedroom master screen; Colleen's face appeared on the screen. He punched for the door release, missed, punched again, caught it. He ran his hands through his hair, snapped the top clip of his coveralls, went to the entrance hall.

Colleen appeared tiny and hesitant standing in the hall. As he saw her, something weblike, decisive, meshed inside him – a completeness.

He thought, *Boy, in just one day you are completely on the hook.*

'Eric,' she said.

Her body's warm softness clung to him. Fragrance wafted from her hair.

'I missed you,' he said.

She pulled away, looked up. 'Did you dream about me?'

He kissed her. 'Just a normal dream.'

'Doctor!'

A smile took the sting out of the exclamation. She pulled away, slipped off her fur-lined cape. From an inner pocket of the cape she extracted a flat blue booklet. 'Here's the diagram. Pete didn't suspect a thing.'

Abruptly, she reeled toward him, clutched at his arm, gasping.

He steadied her, frightened. 'What's the matter, darling?'

She shook her head, drawing deep, shuddering breaths.

'It's nothing; just a . . . little headache.'

'Little headache nothing.' He put the back of his wrist against her forehead. The skin held a feverish warmth. 'Do you feel ill?'

She shook her head. 'No. It's going away.'

'I don't like this as a symptom. Have you eaten?'

She looked up, calmer. 'No, but I seldom eat breakfast . . . the waistline.'

'Nonsense! You come in here and eat some fruit.'

She smiled at him. 'Yes, doctor . . . darling.'

The reflection on the musikron's inner control surfaces gave an underlighted, demoniacal cast to Pete's face. His hand rested on a relay switch. Hesitant thought: *Colleen,*

I wish I could control your thoughts. I wish I could tell you what to do. Each time I try, you get a headache. I wish I knew how this machine really works.

Eric's lab still bore the cluttered look of his night's activities. He helped Colleen up to a seat on the edge of the bench, opened the musikron booklet beside her. She looked down at the open pages.

'What are all those funny looking squiggles?'

He smiled. 'Circuit diagram.' He took a test clip and, glancing at the diagram, began pulling leads from the resonance circuit. He stopped, a puzzled frown drawing down his features. He stared at the diagram. 'That can't be right.' He found a scratch pad, stylus, began checking the booklet.

'What's wrong?'

'This doesn't make sense.'

'How do you mean?'

'It isn't designed for what it's supposed to do.'

'Are you certain?'

'I know Dr Amanti's work. This isn't the way he works.' He began leafing through the booklet. A page flopped loose. He examined the binding. The booklet's pages had been razored out and new pages substituted. It was a good job. If the page hadn't fallen out, he might not have noticed. 'You said it was easy to get this. Where was it?'

'Right out on top of the musikron.'

He stared at her speculatively.

'What's wrong?' Her eyes held open candor.

'I wish I knew.' He pointed to the booklet. 'That thing's as phony as a Martian canal.'

'How do you know?'

'If I put it together that way' – a gesture at the booklet – 'it'd go up in smoke the instant power hit it. There's only one explanation: Pete's on to us.'

'But how?'

'That's what I'd like to know . . . how he anticipated you'd try to get the diagram for me. Maybe that busboy—'

'Tommy? But he's such a nice young fellow.'

'Yeah. He'd sell his mother if the price was right. He could have eavesdropped last night.'

'I can't believe it.' She shook her head.

In the webwork of the musikron, Pete gritted his teeth. *Hate him! Hate him!* He pressed the thought at her, saw it fail. With a violent motion, he jerked the metal hemisphere off his head, stumbled out of the musikron. *You're not going to have her! If it's a dirty fight you want, I'll really show you a dirty fight!*

Colleen asked, 'Isn't there some other explanation?'

'Can you think of one?'

She started to slide down from the bench, hesitated, lurched against him, pressing her head against his chest. 'My head . . . my head—' She went limp in his arms, shuddered, recovered slowly, drew gasping breaths. She stood up. 'Thank you.'

In a corner of the lab was a canvas deck chair. He led her over to it, eased her down. 'You're going to a hospital right now for a complete check-up – tracers, the works. I don't like this.'

'It's just a headache.'

'Peculiar kind of a headache.'

'I'm not going to a hospital.'

'Don't argue. I'm calling for reservations as soon as I can get over to the phone.'

'Eric, I won't do it!' She pushed herself upright in the chair. 'I've seen all the doctors I want to see.' She hesitated, looked up at him. 'Except you. I've had all those tests. There's nothing wrong with me . . . except something in my head.' She smiled. 'I guess I'm talking to the right kind of a doctor for that.'

She lay back resting, closed her eyes. Eric pulled up a stool, sat down beside her, holding her hand. Colleen appeared to sink into a light sleep, breathing evenly. Minutes passed.

If the teleprobe wasn't practically dismantled, I could test her, he thought.

She stirred, opened her eyes.

'It's that musikron,' he said. He took her arm. 'Did you ever have headaches like this before you began working with that thing?'

'I had headaches, but . . . well, they weren't this bad.' She shuddered. 'I kept having horrible dreams last night about all those poor people going insane. I kept waking up. I wanted to go in and have it out with Pete.' She put her hands over her face. 'How can you be certain it's the musikron? You can't be sure. I won't believe it! I can't.'

Eric stood up, went to the bench and rummaged under loose parts for a notebook. He returned, tossed the book into her lap. 'There's your proof.'

She looked at the book without opening it. 'What is this?'

'It's some figures on your itinerary. I had a travel bureau check your departure times. From the time Pete would have been shutting down the musikron to the moment all hell broke loose there's an even twenty-eight-hour time lapse. That same time lag is present in each case.'

She pushed the notebook from her lap. 'I don't believe it. You're making this up.'

He shook his head. 'Colleen, what does it mean to you that you have been each place where the Syndrome hit . . . that there was a twenty-eight-hour time lapse in each case? Isn't that stretching coincidence too far?'

'I know it's not true.' Her lips thinned. 'I don't know what I've been thinking of to even consider you were right.' She looked up, eyes withdrawn. 'It can't be true. If it was, it would mean Pete planned the whole thing. He's just not that kind of a guy. He's nice, thoughtful.'

He started to put his hand on her arm. 'But, Colleen, I thought—'

'Don't touch me. I don't care what you thought, or what I thought. I think you've been using your psychological ability to try to turn me away from Pete.'

He shook his head, again tried to take her arm.

She pulled away. 'No! I want to think and I can't think when . . . when you touch me.' She stared at him. 'I believe you're just jealous of Pete.'

'That's not—'

A motion at the lab door caught his eye, stopped him. Pete stood there, leaning on his cane.

Eric thought, *How did he get there? I didn't hear a thing. How long has he been there?* He stood up.

Pete stepped forward. 'You forgot to latch your door, doctor.' He looked at Colleen. 'Common enough thing. I did too.' He limped into the room, cane tapping methodically. 'You were saying something about jealousy.' A pause. 'I understand about jealousy.'

'Pete!' Colleen stared at him, turned back to Eric. 'Eric, I—' she began, and then shrugged.

Pete rested both hands on his cane, looked up at Eric. 'You weren't going to leave me anything, were you, doctor – the woman I love, the musikron. You were even going to hang me for this Syndrome thing.'

Eric stopped, retrieved his notebook from the floor. He handed it to Pete, who turned it over, looked at the back.

'The proof's in there. There's a twenty-eight-hour time lag between the moment you leave a community and the moment madness breaks out. You already know it's followed you around the world. There's no deviation. I've checked it out.'

Pete's face paled. 'Coincidence. Figures can lie; I'm no monster.'

Colleen turned toward Eric, back to Pete. 'That's what I told him, Pete.'

'Nobody's accusing you of being a monster, Pete . . . yet,' Eric said. 'You *could* be a savior. The knowledge that's locked up in that musikron could practically wipe out insanity. It's a positive link with the unconscious . . . can be tapped any time. Why, properly shielded—'

'Nuts! You're trying to get the musikron so you can throw your weight around.' He looked at Colleen. 'And you sugar-talked her into helping you.' He sneered. 'It's not the first time I've been double-crossed by a woman; I guess I should've been a psychiatrist.'

Colleen shook her head. 'Pete, don't talk that way.'

'Yeah . . . How else do you expect me to talk? You were a nobody; a canary in a hula chorus and I picked you up and set you down right on the top. So what do you do—' He turned away, leaning heavily on the cane. 'You can have her, Doc; she's just your type!'

Eric put out a hand, withdrew it. 'Pete! Stop allowing your deformity to deform your reason! It doesn't matter how we feel about Colleen. We've got to think about what the musikron is doing to people! Think of all the unhappiness this is causing people . . . the death . . . the pain—'

'People!' Pete spat out the word.

Eric took a step closer to him. 'Stop that! You know I'm right. You can have full credit for anything that is developed. You can have full control of it. You can—'

'Don't try to kid me, Doc. It's been tried by experts. You and your big words! You're just trying to make a big impression on baby here. I already told you you can have her. I don't want her.'

'Pete! You—'

'Look out, Doc; you're losing your temper!'

'Who wouldn't in the face of your pig-headedness?'

'So it's pig-headed to fight a thief, eh, Doc?' Pete spat on the floor, turned toward the door, tripped on his cane and fell.

Colleen was at his side. 'Pete, are you hurt?'

He pushed her away. 'I can take care of myself!' He struggled to his feet, pulling himself up on the cane.

'Pete, please—'

Eric saw moisture in Pete's eyes. 'Pete, let's solve this thing.'

'It's already solved, Doc.' He limped through the doorway.

Colleen hesitated. 'I have to go with him. I can't let him go away like this. There's no telling what he'll do.'

'But don't you see what he's doing?'

Anger flamed in her eyes; she stared at Eric. 'I saw what you did and it was as cruel a thing as I've ever seen.' She turned and ran after Pete.

Her footsteps drummed up the stairs; the outer door slammed.

An empty fibreboard box lay on the floor beside the teleprobe. Eric kicked it across the lab.

'Unreasonable . . . neurotic . . . flighty . . . irresponsible—'

He stopped; emptiness grew in his chest. He looked at the teleprobe. 'Sometimes, there's no predicting about women.' He went to the bench, picked up a transistor, put it down, pushed a tumble of resistors to the back of the bench.. 'Should've known better.'

He turned, started toward the door, froze with a thought which forced out all other awareness:

What if they leave Seattle?

He ran up the stairs three at a time, out the door, stared up and down the street. A jet car sped past with a single occupant. A woman and two children approached from his left. Otherwise, the street was empty. The unitube entrance, less than half a block away, disgorged three teen-age girls. He started toward them, thought better of it. With the tubes running fifteen seconds apart, his chance to catch them had been lost while he'd nursed his hurt.

He re-entered the apartment.

I have to do something, he thought. *If they leave, Seattle will go the way of all the others.* He sat down by the vidiphone, put his finger in the dial, withdrew it.

If I call the police, they'll want proof. What can I show them besides some time-tables? He looked out the window at his left. *The musikron! They'll see—* Again he reached for the dial, again withdrew. *What would they see? Pete would just claim I was trying to steal it.*

He stood up, paced to the window, stared out at the lake.

I could call the society, he thought.

He ticked off in his mind the current top officers of the King County Society of Psychiatric Consultants. All of them considered Dr Eric Ladde a little too successful for one so young; and besides there was the matter of his research on the teleprobe; mostly a laughable matter.

But I have to do something . . . the Syndrome— He shook his head. *I'll have to do it alone, whatever I do.* He slipped into a black cape, went outside and headed for the Gweduc Room.

A cold wind kicked up whitecaps in the bay, plumed spray onto the waterfront sidewalk. Eric ducked into the elevator, emerged into a lunchroom atmosphere. The girl at the checktable looked up.

'Are you alone, doctor?'

'I'm looking for Miss Lanai.'

'I'm sorry. You must have passed them outside. She and Mr Serantis just left.'

'Do you know where they were going?'

'I'm sorry; perhaps if you come back this evening—'

Eric returned to the elevator, rode up to the street vaguely disquieted. As he emerged from the elevator dome, he saw a van pull away from the service dome. Eric played a hunch, ran toward the service elevator which already was whirring down.

'Hey!'

The whirring stopped, resumed; the elevator returned to the street level, in it Tommy, the busboy.

'Better luck next time, Doc.'

'Where are they?'

'Well—'

Eric jammed a hand into his coin pocket, fished out a fifty-buck piece, held it in his hand.

Tommy looked at the coin, back at Eric's eyes. 'I heard Pete call the Bellingham skytrain field for reservations to London.'

A hard knot crept into Eric's stomach; his breathing became shallow, quick; he looked around him.

'Only twenty-eight hours—'

'That's all I know, Doc.'

Eric looked at the busboy's eyes, studying him.

Tommy shook his head. 'Don't you start looking at me that way!' He shuddered. 'That Pete give me the creeps; always staring at a guy; sitting around in that machine all day and no noises coming out of it.' Again he shuddered. 'I'm glad he's gone.'

Eric handed him the coin. 'You won't be.'

'Yeah,' Tommy stepped back into the elevator. 'Sorry you didn't make it with the babe, Doc.'

'Wait.'

'Yeah?'

'Wasn't there a message from Miss Lanai?'

Tommy made an almost imperceptible motion toward the inner pocket of his coveralls. Eric's trained eyes caught the gesture. He stepped forward, gripped Tommy's arm.

'Give it to me!'

'Now look here, Doc.'

'Give it to me!'

'Doc, I don't know what you're talking about.'

Eric pushed his face close to the busboy's. 'Did you see what happened to Los Angeles, Lawton, Portland, all the places where the Syndrome hit?'

The boy's eyes went wide. 'Doc, I—'

'Give it to me!'

Tommy darted his free hand under his coveralls, extracted a thick envelope, thrust it into Eric's hand.

Eric released the boy's arm. Scrawled on the envelope was: 'This will prove you were wrong about Pete.' It was signed, 'Colleen.'

'You were going to keep this?' Eric asked.

Tommy's lips twisted. 'Any fool can see it's the plans for the musikron, Doc. That thing's valuable.'

'You haven't any idea,' Eric said. He looked up. 'They're headed for Bellingham?'

'Yeah.'

The nonstop unitube put Eric at the Bellingham field in twenty-one minutes. He jumped out, ran to the station, jostling people aside. A skytrain lashed into the air at the far end of the field. Eric missed a step, stumbled, caught his balance.

In the depot, people streamed past him away from the ticket window. Eric ran up to the window, leaned on the counter. 'Next train to London?'

The girl at the window consulted a screen beside her. 'There'll be one at 12:50 tomorrow afternoon, sir. You just missed one.'

'But that's twenty-four hours!'

'You'd arrive in London at 4:50pm, sir.' She smiled. 'Just a little late for tea.' She glanced at his caduceus.

Eric clutched at the edge of the counter, leaned toward her. 'That's twenty-nine hours – one hour too late.'

He pushed himself away from the window, turned.

'It's *just* a four-hour trip, doctor.'

He turned back. 'Can I charter a private ship?'

'Sorry, doctor. There's an electrical storm coming; the traveler beam will have to be shut down. I'm sure you couldn't get a pilot to go out without the beam. You do understand?'

'Is there a way to call someone on the skytrain?'

'Is this a personal matter, doctor?'

'It's an emergency.'

'May I ask the nature of the emergency?'

He thought a moment, looking at the girl. He thought, *Same problem here . . . nobody would believe me.*

He said, 'Never mind. Where's the nearest vidiphone? I'll leave a message for her at Plymouth Depot.'

'Down that hallway to your right, doctor.' The girl went back to her tickets. She looked up at Eric's departing back. 'Was it a medical emergency, doctor?'

He paused, turned. The envelope in his pocket rustled. He felt for the papers, pulled out the envelope. For the second time since Tommy had given them to him, Eric glanced inside at the folded pages of electronic diagrams, some initialed 'CA.'

The girl waited, staring at him.

Eric put the envelope back in his pocket, a thought crystalizing. He glanced up at the girl. 'Yes, it was a medical emergency. But you're out of range.'

He turned, strode outside, back to the unitube. He thought about Colleen. *Never trust a neurotic woman. I should have known better than to let my glands hypnotize me.*

He went down the unitube entrance, worked his way out to the speed strip, caught the first car along, glad to find it empty. He took out the envelope, examined its contents during the ride. There was no doubt about it; the envelope contained the papers Pete had razored from the musikron service book. Eric recognized Dr Amanti's characteristic scrawl.

The wall clock in his lab registered 2:10pm as Eric turned on the lights. He took a blank sheet of paper from his notebook, wrote on it with grease pencil:

'DEADLINE, 4:00pm, Sunday, May 16th.'

He tacked the sheet above his bench, spread out the circuit diagrams from the envelope. He examined the first page.

Series modulation, he thought. *Quarter wave.* He ran a stylus down the page, checked the next page. *Multiple phase-reversing.* He turned to the next page. The stylus paused. He traced a circuit, went back to the first page. *Degenerative feedback.* He shook his head. *That's impossible! There'd just be a maze of wild harmonics.* He continued on through the diagrams, stopped and read through the last two pages slowly. He went through the circuits a second time, a third time, a fourth time. He shook his head. *What is it?*

He could trace the projection of much of the diagram, amazed at the clear simplicity of the ideas. The last ten pages though— They described a series of faintly familiar

circuits, reminding him of a dual frequency crystal cali-
brator of extremely high oscillation. '10,000 KC' was
marked in the margin. But there were subtle differences
he couldn't explain. For instance, there was a sign for a
lower limit.

A series of them, he thought. *The harmonics hunt and
change. But it can't be random. Something has to control
it, balance it.*

At the foot of the last page was a notation: 'Important
– use only C6 midget variable, C7, C8 dual, 4ufd.'

They haven't made tubes in that series for fifty years,
he thought. *How can I substitute?*

He studied the diagram.

*I don't stand a chance of making this thing in time.
And if I do; what then?* He wiped his forehead. *Why does
it remind me of a crystal oscillator?* He looked at the
clock – two hours had passed. *Where did the time go?* he
asked himself. *I'm taking too much time just learning what
this is.* He chewed his lips, staring at the moving second
hand of the clock, suddenly froze. *The parts houses will
be closing and tomorrow's Sunday!*

He went to the lab vidiphone, dialed a parts house. No
luck. He dialed another, checking the call sheet beside
the phone. No luck. His fifth call netted a suggestion of a
substitute circuit using transistors which might work. Eric
checked off the parts list the clerk suggested, gave the man
his package tube code.

'I'll have them out to you first thing Monday,' the
man said.

'But I have to have them today! Tonight!'

'I'm sorry, sir. The parts are in our warehouse; it's all
locked up tight on Saturday afternoon.'

'I'll pay a hundred bucks above list price for those
parts.'

'I'm sorry, sir; I don't have authorization.'

'Two hundred.'

'But—'

'Three hundred.'

The clerk hesitated. Eric could see the man figuring. The three hundred probably was a week's wages.

'I'll have to get them myself after I go off duty here,' the clerk said. 'What else do you need?'

Eric leafed through the circuit diagrams, read off the parts list from the margins. 'There's another hundred bucks in it if you get them to me before seven.'

'I get off at 5:30, doctor. I'll do my best.'

Eric broke the circuit, returned to his bench, began roughing-in from the diagram with what materials he had. The teleprobe formed the basic element with surprisingly few changes.

At 5:40, the dropbell of his transgraph jangled upstairs. Eric put down his soldering iron, went upstairs, pulled out the tape. His hands trembled when he saw the transmission station. London. He read:

'Don't ever try to see me again. Your suspicions are entirely unfounded as you probably know by now. Pete and I to be married Monday. Colleen.'

He sat down at the transmitter, punched out a message to American Express, coding it urgent for delivery to Colleen Lanai.

'Colleen: If you can't think of me, please think of what this means to a city full of people. Bring Pete and that machine back before it's too late. You can't be this inhuman.'

He hesitated before signing it, punched out, 'I love you.' He signed it, 'Eric.'

He thought, *You damn' fool, Eric. After the way she ran out on you.*

He went into the kitchen, took a capsule to stave off weariness, ate a dinner of pills, drank a cup of coffee. He leaned back against the kitchen drainboard, waiting for the capsule to take hold. His head cleared; he washed his face in cold water, dried it, returned to the lab.

The front door announcer chimed at 6:42pm. The screen showed the clerk from the parts house, his arms gripping a bulky package. Eric punched the door release, spoke into the tube: 'First door on your left, downstairs.'

The back wall of his bench suddenly wavered, the lines of masonry rippling; a moment of disorientation surged through him. He bit his lip, holding to the reality of the pain.

It's too soon, he thought. *Probably my own nerves; I'm too tense.*

An idea on the nature of the Syndrome flashed into his mind. He pulled a scratch pad to him, scribbled, 'Loss of unconscious autonomy; overstimulation subliminal receptors; gross perception – petit perception. Check C. G. Jung's collective unconscious.'

Footsteps tapped down the stairway.

'This the place?'

The clerk was a taller man than he had expected. An air of near adolescent eagerness played across the man's features as he took in the lab. 'What a layout!'

Eric cleared a space on the bench. 'Put that stuff right here.' Eric's eyes focused on the clerk's delicately sensitive hands. The man slid the box onto the bench, picked up a fixed crystal oscillator from beside the box, examined it.

'Do you know anything about electronic hookups?' Eric asked.

The clerk looked up, grinned. 'W7CGO. I've had my own ham station over ten years.'

Eric offered his hand. 'I'm Dr Eric Ladde.'

'Baldwin Platte . . . Baldy.' He ran one of his sensitive hands through thinning hair.

'Glad to know you, Baldy. How'd you like to make a thousand bucks over what I've already promised you?'

'Are you kidding, Doc?'

Eric turned his head, looked at the framework of the teleprobe. 'If that thing isn't finished and ready to go by four o'clock tomorrow afternoon, Seattle will go the way of Los Angeles.'

Baldy's eyes widened; he looked at the framework. 'The Syndrome? How can—'

'I've discovered what caused the Syndrome . . . a machine like this. I have to build a copy of that machine and get it working. Otherwise—'

The clerk's eyes were clear, sober. 'I saw your nameplate upstairs, Doc, and remembered I'd read about you.'

'Well?'

'If you say positive you've found out what caused the Syndrome, I'll take your word for it. Just don't try to explain it to me.' He looked toward the parts on the bench, back to the teleprobe. 'Tell me what I'm supposed to do.' A pause. 'And I hope you know what you're talking about.'

'I've found something that just can't be coincidence,' Eric said. 'Added to what I know about teleprobes, well—' He hesitated. 'Yes, I know what I'm talking about.'

Eric took a small bottle from the rear of his bench, looked at the label, shook out a capsule. 'Here, take this; it'll keep you awake.'

Baldy swallowed the capsule.

Eric sorted through the papers on his bench, found the first sheet. 'Now, here's what we're dealing with. There's a tricky quarter-wave hookup coupled to an amplification factor that'll throw you back on your heels.'

Baldy looked over Eric's shoulder. 'Doesn't look too hard to follow. Let me work on that while you take over some of the tougher parts.' He reached for the diagram, moved it to a cleared corner of the bench. 'What's this thing supposed to do, Doc?'

'It creates a field of impulses which feed directly into the human unconscious. The field distorts—'

Baldy interrupted him. 'OK, Doc. I forgot I asked you not to explain it to me.' He looked up, smiled. 'I flunked Sociology.' His expression sobered. 'I'll just work on the assumption you know what this is all about. Electronics I understand; psychology . . . no.'

* * *

They worked in silence, broken only by sparse questions, muttering. The second hand on the wall clock moved around, around, around; the minute hand followed, and the hour hand.

At 8:00am, they sent out for breakfast. The layout of the crystal oscillators still puzzled them. Much of the diagram was scrawled in a radio shorthand.

Baldy made the first break in the puzzle.

'Doc, are these things supposed to make a noise?'

Eric looked at the diagram. 'What?' His eyes widened. 'Of course they're supposed to make a noise.'

Baldy wet his lips with his tongue. 'There's a special sonar crystal set for depth sounding in submarine detection. This looks faintly like the circuit, but there are some weird changes.'

Eric tugged at his lip; his eyes glistened. 'That's it! That's why there's no control circuit! That's why it looks as though these things would hunt all over the place! The operator is the control – his mind keeps it in balance!'

'How's that?'

Eric ignored the question. 'But this means we have the wrong kind of crystals. We've misread the parts list.' Frustration sagged his shoulders. 'And we're not even halfway finished.'

Baldy tapped the diagram with a finger. 'Doc, I've got some old surplus sonar equipment at home. I'll call my wife and have her bring it over. I think there are six or seven sonopulsators – they just might work.'

Eric looked at the wall clock: 8:28am. Seven and a half hours to go. 'Tell her to hurry.'

Mrs 'Baldy' was a female version of her husband. She carried a heavy wooden box down the steps, balancing it with an easy nonchalance.

'Hi, Hon. Where'll I put this stuff?'

'On the floor . . . anywhere. Doc, this is Betty.'

'How do you do.'

'Hiya, Doc. There's some more stuff in the car. I'll get it.'

Baldy took her arm. 'You better let me do it. You shouldn't be carrying heavy loads, especially down stairs.'

She pulled away. 'Go on. Get back to your work. This is good for me – I need the exercise.'

'But—'

'But me no buts.' She pushed him.

He returned to the bench reluctantly, looking back at his wife. She turned at the doorway and looked at Baldy. 'You look pretty good for being up all night, Hon. What's all the rush?'

'I'll explain later. You better get that stuff.'

Baldy turned to the box she had brought, began sorting through it. 'Here they are.' He lifted out two small plastic cases, handed them to Eric, pulled out another, another. There were eight of them. They lined the cases up on the bench. Baldy snapped open the cover of the first one.

'They're mostly printed circuits, crystal diode transistors and a few tubes. Wonderful engineering. Don't know what the dickens I ever planned to do with them. Couldn't resist the bargain. They were two bucks apiece.' He folded back the side plate. 'Here's the crys— Doc!'

Eric bent over the case.

Baldy reached into the case. 'What were those tubes you wanted?'

Eric grabbed the circuit diagram, ran his finger down the parts list. 'C6 midget variable, C7, C8 dual, 4ufd.'

Baldy pulled out a tube. 'There's your C6.' He pulled out another. 'There's your C8.' Another. 'Your C7.' He peered into the works. 'There's a third stage in here I don't think'll do us any good. We can rig a substitute for the 4ufd component.'

Baldy whistled tonelessly through his teeth. 'No wonder that diagram looked familiar. It was based on this wartime circuit.'

Eric felt a moment of exultation, sobered when he looked at the wall clock: 9:04am.

He thought, *We have to work faster or we'll never make it in time. Less than seven hours to go.*

He said, 'Let's get busy. We haven't much time.'

Betty came down the stairs with another box. 'You guys eaten?'

Baldy didn't look up from dismantling the second plastic box. 'Yeah, but you might make us some sandwiches for later.'

Eric looked up from another of the plastic boxes. 'Cupboard upstairs is full of food.'

Betty turned, clattered up the stairs.

Baldy glanced at Eric out of the corners of his eyes. 'Doc, don't say anything to Betty about the reason for all this.' He turned his attention back to the box, working methodically. 'We're expecting our first son in about five months.' He took a deep breath. 'You've got me convinced.' A drop of perspiration ran down his nose, fell onto his hand. He wiped his hand on his shirt. 'This has gotta work.'

Betty's voice echoed down the stairs: 'Hey, Doc, where's your can opener?'

Eric had his head and shoulders inside the teleprobe. He pulled back, shouted, 'Motor-punch to the left of the sink.'

Muttering, grumbling, clinking noises echoed down from the kitchen. Presently, Betty appeared with a plate of sandwiches, a red-tinted bandage on her left thumb. 'Broke your paring knife,' she said. 'Those mechanical gadgets scare me.' She looked fondly at her husband's back. 'He's just as gadget happy as you are, Doc. If I didn't watch him like a spy-beam my nice old kitchen would be an electronic nightmare.' She upended an empty box, put the plate of sandwiches on it. 'Eat when you get hungry. Anything I can do?'

Baldy stepped back from the bench, turned. 'Why don't you go over to Mom's for the day?'

'The whole day?'

Baldy glanced at Eric, back at his wife. 'The Doc's

paying me fourteen hundred bucks for the day's work. That's our baby money; now run along.'

She made as though to speak, closed her mouth, walked over to her husband, kissed his cheek. 'OK, Hon. Bye.' She left.

Eric and Baldy went on with their work, the pressure mounting with each clock tick. They plodded ahead, methodically checking each step.

At 3:20pm, Baldy released test clips from half of the new resonance circuit, glanced at the wall clock. He stopped, looked back at the teleprobe, weighing the work yet to be done. Eric lay on his back under the machine, soldering a string of new connections.

'Doc, we aren't going to make it.' He put the test meter on the bench, leaned against the bench. 'There just isn't enough time.'

An electronic soldering iron skidded out from under the teleprobe. Eric squirmed out behind it, looked up at the clock, back at the unconnected wires of the crystal circuits. He stood up, fished a credit book from his pocket, wrote out a fourteen hundred buck credit check to Baldwin Platte. He tore out the check, handed it to Baldy.

'You've earned every cent of this, Baldy. Now beat it; go join your wife.'

'But—'

'We haven't time to argue. Lock the door after you so you can't get back in if—'

Baldy raised his right hand, dropped it. 'Doc, I can't—'

'It's all right, Baldy.' Eric took a deep breath. 'I kind of know how I'll go if I'm too late.' He stared at Baldy. 'I don't know about you. You might, well—' He shrugged.

Baldy nodded, swallowed. 'I guess you're right, Doc.' His lips worked. Abruptly, he turned, ran up the stairs. The outside door slammed.

Eric turned back to the teleprobe, picked up an open lead to the crystal circuits, matched it to its receptor, ran a drop of solder across the connection. He moved to the next crystal unit, the next—

At one minute to four he looked at the clock. More than an hour's work remained on the teleprobe and then— He didn't know. He leaned back against the bench, eyes filmed by fatigue. He pulled a cigarette from his pocket, pressed the igniter, took a deep drag. He remembered Colleen's question: 'What's it like to be insane?' He stared at the ember on his cigarette.

Will I tear the teleprobe apart? Will I take a gun, go hunting for Colleen and Pete? Will I run out— The clock behind him clicked. He tensed. *What will it be like?* He felt dizzy, nauseated. A wave of melancholia smothered his emotions. Tears of self-pity started in his eyes. He gritted his teeth. *I'm not insane . . . I'm not insane—* He dug his fingernails into his palms, drew in deep, shuddering breaths. Uncertain thoughts wandered through his mind.

I shall faint . . . the incoherence of morosis . . . demoniacal possession . . . dithyrambic dizziness . . . an anima figure concretionized out of the libido . . . corybantic calenture . . . mad as a March hare—

His head sagged forward.

. . . Non compos mentis . . . aliéné . . . avoir le diable au corps— What has happened to Seattle? What has happened to Seattle? What has— His breathing steadied; he blinked his eyes. Everything appeared unchanged . . . unchanged . . . unchanged— *I'm wandering. I must get hold of myself!*

The fingers of his right hand burned. He shook away the short ember of his cigarette.

Was I wrong? What's happening outside? He started for the stairs, made it halfway to the door when the lights went out. A tight band ringed his chest. Eric felt his way to the door, grasped the stair rail, climbed up to the dim, filtered light of the hall. He stared at the stained glass bricks beside the door, tensed at a burst of gunshots from outside. He sleepwalked to the kitchen, raised on tiptoes to look through the ventilator window over the sink.

People! The street swarmed with people—some running, some walking purposefully, some wandering without aim, some clothed, some partly clothed, some nude. The bodies of a man and child sprawled in blood at the opposite curbing.

He shook his head, turned, went into the living room. The lights suddenly flashed on, off, on, stayed. He punched video for a news program, got only wavy lines. He put the set on manual, dialed a Tacoma station. Again wavy lines.

Olympia was on the air, a newscaster reading a weather report: 'Partly cloudy with showers by tomorrow afternoon. Temperatures—'

A hand carrying a sheet of paper reached into the speaker's field of vision. The newsman stopped, scanned the paper. His hand shook. 'Attention! Our mobile unit at the Clyde Field jet races reports that the Scramble Syndrome has struck the twin cities of Seattle–Tacoma. More than three million people are reported infected. Emergency measures already are being taken. Road blocks are being set up. There are known to have been fatalities, but—'

A new sheet of paper was handed to the announcer. His jaw muscles twitched as he read. 'A jet racer has crashed into the crowd at Clyde Field. The death toll is estimated at three hundred. There are no available medical facilities. All doctors listening to this broadcast – all doctors – report at once to State disaster headquarters. Emergency medical —' The lights again blinked out, the screen faded.

Eric hesitated. *I'm a doctor. Shall I go outside and do what I can, medically, or shall I go down and finish the teleprobe – now that I've been proved right? Would it do any good if I did get it working?* He found himself breathing in a deep rhythm. *Or am I crazed like all the others? Am I really doing what I think I'm doing? Am I mad and dreaming a reality?* He thought of pinching himself, knew that would be no proof. *I have to go ahead as though I'm sane. Anything else* really *is madness.*

He chose the teleprobe, located a handlight in his bedroom, returned to the basement lab. He found the long unused emergency generator under the crates in the corner. He wheeled it to the center of the lab, examined it. The powerful alcohol turbine appeared in working order. The pressure cap on the fuel reservoir popped as he released it. The reservoir was more than half full. He found two carboys of alcohol fuel in the corner where the generator had been stored. He filled the fuel tank, replaced the cap, pumped pressure into the tank.

The generator's power lead he plugged into the lab fuse box. The hand igniter caught on the first spin. The turbine whirred to life, keened up through the sonic range. Lab lights sprang to life, dimmed, steadied as the relays adjusted.

It was 7:22pm by the wall clock when he soldered the final connection. Eric estimated a half hour delay before the little generator had taken over, put the time actually at near eight o'clock. He found himself hesitant, strangely unwilling to test the completed machine. His one-time encephalorecorder was a weird maze of crossed wiring, emergency shielding, crowded tubes, crystals. The only familiar thing remaining in the tubular framework was the half-dome of the head-contact hanging above the test chair.

Eric plugged in a power line, linked it to a portable switchbox which he placed in the machine beside the chair. He eased aside a sheaf of wires, wormed his way through, sat down in the chair. He hesitated, hand on the switch.

Am I really sitting here? he wondered. *Or is this some trick of the unconscious mind? Perhaps I'm in a corner somewhere with a thumb in my mouth. Maybe I've torn the teleprobe apart. Maybe I've put the teleprobe together so it will kill me the instant I close the switch.*

He looked down at the switch, withdrew his hand. He thought, *I can't just sit here; that's madness, too.*

He reached up to the helmetlike dome, brought it down over his head. He felt the pinpricks of the contacts as they probed through his hair to his scalp. The narco-needles took hold, deadening skin sensation.

This feels like reality, he thought. *But maybe I'm building this out of memory. It's hardly likely I'm the only sane person in the city.* He lowered his hand to the switch. *But I have to act as though I am.*

Almost of its own volition, his thumb moved, depressed the switch. Instantly, a soft ululation hung in the laboratory air. It shifted to dissonance, to harmony, wailing, half-forgotten music, wavered up the scale, down the scale.

In Eric's mind, mottled pictures of insanity threatened to overwhelm his consciousness. He sank into a maelstrom. A brilliant spectrograph coruscated before his eyes. In a tiny corner of his awareness, a discrete pattern of sensation remained, a reality to hold onto, to save him – the feeling of the teleprobe's chair beneath him and against his back.

He sank farther into the maelstrom, saw it change to gray, become suddenly a tiny picture seen through the wrong end of a telescope. He saw a small boy holding the hand of a woman in a black dress. The two went into a hall-like room. Abruptly Eric no longer saw them from a distance but was again himself at age nine walking toward a casket. He sensed again the horrified fascination, heard his mother's sobs, the murmurous, meaningless voice sounds of a tall, thin undertaker. Then, there was the casket and in it a pale, waxed creature who looked somewhat like his father. As Eric watched, the face melted and became the face of his uncle Mark; and then another mask, his high-school geometry teacher. Eric thought, *We missed that one in my psychoanalysis.* He watched the mobile face in the coffin as it again shifted and became the professor who had taught him abnormal psychology, and then his own analyst, Dr Lincoln Ordway, and then – he fought against this one – Dr Carlos Amanti.

So that's the father image I've held all these years, he thought. *That means— That means I've never really given up searching for my father. A fine thing for an analyst to discover about himself!* He hesitated. *Why did I have to recognize that? I wonder if Pete went through this in his musikron?* Another part of his mind said, *Of course not. A person has to want to see inside himself or he never will, even if he has the opportunity.*

The other part of his mind abruptly seemed to reach up, seize control of his consciousness. His awareness of self lurched aside, became transformed into a mote whipping through his memories so rapidly he could barely distinguish between events.

Am I dying? he wondered. *Is it my life passing in review?*

The kaleidoscopic progression jerked to a stop before a vision of Colleen – the way he had seen her in his dream. The memory screen lurched to Pete. He saw the two people in a relationship to himself that he had never quite understood. They represented a catalyst, not good or evil, merely a reagent which set events in motion.

Suddenly, Eric sensed his awareness growing, permeating his body. He knew the condition and action of each gland, each muscle fiber, each nerve ending. He focused his inner eye on the grayness through which he had passed. Into the gray came a tendril of red – shifting, twisting, weaving past him. He followed the red line. A picture formed in his mind, growing there like the awakening from anaesthetic. He looked down a long street – dim in the spring dusk – at the lights of a jet car thundering toward him. The car grew larger, larger, the lights two hypnotic eyes. With the vision came a thought: *My, that's pretty!*

Involuntary reactions took over. He sensed muscles tensing, jumping aside, the hot blast of the jet car as it passed. A plaintive thought twisted into his mind: *Where am I? Where's Mama? Where's Bea?*

Tightness gripped Eric's stomach as he realized he sat in another's consciousness, saw through another's eyes, sensed through another's nerves. He jumped away from the experience, pulling out of the other mind as though he had touched a hot stove.

So that's how Pete knew so much, he thought. *Pete sat in his musikron and looked through our eyes.* Another thought: *What am I doing here?* He sensed the teleprobe chair beneath him, heard the new self within him say, 'I'm going to need more trained, expert help.'

He followed another red tendril, searching, discarded it; sought another. The orientation was peculiar – no precise up or down or compass points until he looked out of the other eyes. He came to rest finally behind two eyes that looked down from an open window in the fortieth story of an office building, sensed the suicidal thoughts building up pressure within this person. Gently, Eric touched the center of consciousness, seeking the name – Dr Lincoln Ordway, psychoanalyst.

Eric thought, *Even now I turn back to my own analyst.*

Tensely, Eric retreated to a lower level of the other's consciousness, knowing that the slightest misstep would precipitate this man's death wish, a jump through that window. The lower levels suddenly erupted a pinwheel of coruscating purple light. The pinwheel slowed, became a mandala figure – at the four points of the figure an open window, a coffin, a transitus-tree and a human face which Eric suddenly recognized as a distorted picture of himself. The face was boyish, slightly vacant.

Eric thought, *The analyst, too, is tied to what he believes is his patient.* With the thought, he willed himself to move gently, unobtrusively into the image of himself, began to expand his area of dominion over the other's unconscious. He pushed a tentative thought against the almost palpable wall which represented Dr Ordway's focus of consciousness: *Linc* (a whisper), *don't jump. Do you hear me, Linc? Don't jump. The city needs your help.*

With part of his mind, Eric realized that if the analyst sensed his mental privacy being invaded that realization could tip the balance, send the man plunging out the window. Another part of Eric's mind took that moment to render up a solution to why he needed this man and others like him: The patterns of insanity broadcast by Pete Serantis could only be counterbalanced by a rebroadcast of calmness and sanity.

Eric tensed, withdrew slightly as he felt the analyst move closer to the window. In the other's mind, he whispered, 'Come away from the window. Come away—' Resistance! A white light expanded in Eric's thoughts, rejected him. He felt himself swimming out into the gray maelstrom, receding. A red tendril approached and with it a question, not of his own origin, lifted into his mind:

Eric? What is this thing?

Eric allowed the pattern of teleprobe development to siphon through his mind. He ended the pattern with an explanation of what was needed.

Thought: *Eric, how did the Syndrome miss you?*

Conditioning by long exposure to my own teleprobe; high resistance to unconscious distortion built up by that work.

Funny thing; I was about to dive out the window when I sensed your interference. It was something – the red tendril moved closer – *like this.*

They meshed completely.

'What now?' asked Dr Ordway.

'We'll need as much trained help as we can find in the city. Others would censor out this experience below the threshold of consciousness.'

'The influence of your teleprobe may quiet everybody.'

'Yes, but if the machine is ever turned off, or if people go beyond its area of influence, they'd be back in the soup.'

'We'll have to go in the back door of every unconscious in the city and put things in order!'

'Not just *this* city; every city where the musikron has been and every city where Serantis takes it until we can stop him.'

'How did the musikron do this thing?'

Eric projected a mixed pattern of concepts and pictures: 'The musikron pushed us deep down into the collective unconscious, dangled us there as long as we remained within its area of influence. (Picture of rope hanging down into swirls of fog.) Then the musikron was turned off. (Picture of knife cutting the rope, the end falling into a swirling gray maelstrom.) Do you see it?'

'If we have to go down into that maelstrom after all these people, hadn't we better get started?'

He was a short man digging with his fingers in the soft loam of his flowerbed, staring vacantly at shredded leaves – name, Dr Harold Marsh, psychologist. Unobtrusively, softly, they absorbed him into the network of the teleprobe.

She was a woman, dressed in a thin housecoat, preparing to leap from the end of a pier – name, Lois Voorhies, lay analyst. Swiftly, they drew her back to sanity.

Eric paused to follow a thin red tendril to the mind of a neighbor, saw through the other's eyes sanity returning around him.

Like ripples spreading in a pond, a semblance of sanity washed out across the city. Electric power returned; emergency services were restored.

The eyes of a clinical psychologist east of the city transmitted a view of a jet plane arrowing toward Clyde Field. Through the psychologist's mind the network picked up the radiating thought patterns of a woman – guilt, remorse, despair.

Colleen!

Hesitantly, the network extended a pseudopod of thought, reached into Colleen's consciousness and found terror. *What is happening to me!*

Eric took over. *Colleen, don't be afraid. This is Eric. We are getting things back in order thanks to you and the musikron plans.* He projected the pattern of their accomplishments.

I don't understand. You're—

You don't have to understand now. Hesitantly: *I'm glad you came.*

Eric, I came as soon as I heard – when I realized you

were right about Pete and the musikron. She paused. *We're coming down to land.*

Colleen's chartered plane settled onto the runway, rolled up to a hangar and was surrounded by National Guardsmen.

She sent out a thought: *We have to do something about London. Pete threatened to smash the musikron, to commit suicide. He tried to keep me there by force.*

When?

Six hours ago.

Has it been that long since the Syndrome hit?

The network moved in: *What is the nature of this man Serantis?*

Colleen and Eric merged thoughts to project Pete's personality.

The network: *He'll not commit suicide, or smash his machine. Too self-centered. He'll go into hiding. We'll find him soon enough when we need him – unless he's lynched first.*

Colleen interrupted: *This National Guard major won't let me leave the airport.*

Tell him you're a nurse assigned to Maynard Hospital.

Individual thought from the network: *I'll confirm from this end.*

Eric: *Hurry . . . darling. We need all of the help we can get from people resistant to the teleprobe.*

Thoughts from the network: *That's as good a rationalization as any. Every man to his own type of insanity. That's enough nonsense – let's get to work!*

OCCUPATION FORCE

He was a long time awakening. There was a pounding somewhere. General Henry A. Llewellyn's eyes snapped open. Someone at his bedroom door. Now he heard the voice. 'Sir . . . sir . . . sir . . . ' It was his orderly.

'All right, Watkins, I'm awake.'

The pounding ceased.

He swung his feet out of the bed, looked at the luminous dial on his alarm clock – two-twenty-five. What the devil? He slipped on a robe, a tall, ruddy-faced man – chairman of the Joint Chiefs of Staff.

Watkins saluted when the general opened the door. 'Sir, the President has called an emergency cabinet meeting.' The orderly began to talk faster, his words running all together. 'There's an alien spaceship big as Lake Erie sailing around the earth and getting ready to attack.'

It took a second for the general to interpret the words. He snorted. Pulp magazine poppycock! he thought.

'Sir,' said Watkins, 'there is a staff car downstairs ready to take you to the White House.'

'Get me a cup of coffee while I dress,' said the general.

Representatives of five foreign nations, every cabinet officer, nine senators, fourteen representatives, the heads of the secret service, FBI and of all the armed services were at the meeting. They gathered in the conference room of the White House bomb shelter – a paneled room with paintings around the walls in deep frames to simulate windows. General Llewellyn sat across the oak conference table from the President. The buzzing of voices in the room stopped as the President rapped his gavel. An aide stood up, gave them the first briefing.

A University of Chicago astronomer had picked up the ship at about eight pm. It was coming from the general

194

direction of the belt of Orion. The astronomer had alerted other observatories and someone had thought to notify the government.

The ship had arrowed in at an incredible rate, swung into a one-and-one-half-hour orbit around Earth. It was visible to the unaided eye by that time, another moon. Estimates put its size at nineteen miles long, twelve miles wide, vaguely egg-shaped.

Spectroscopic analysis showed the drive was a hydrogen ion stream with traces of carbon, possibly from the refractor. The invader was transparent to radar, responded to no form of communication.

Majority opinion: a hostile ship on a mission to conquer Earth.

Minority opinion: a *cautious* visitor from space.

Approximately two hours after it took up orbit, the ship put out a five-hundred-foot scout which swooped down on Boston, grappled up a man by the name of William R. Jones from a group of night workers waiting for a bus.

Some of the minority went over to the majority. The President, however, continued to veto all suggestions that they attack. He was supported by the foreign representatives who were in periodic communication with their governments.

'Look at the size of the thing,' said the President. 'An ant with an ant-size pea-shooter could attack an elephant with the same hopes of success we would have.'

'There's always the possibility they're just being prudent,' said a State Department aide. 'We've no evidence they're dissecting this Jones from Boston, as I believe someone suggested.'

'The size precludes peaceful intent,' said General Llewellyn. 'There's an invasion army in that thing. We should fire off every atomic warhead rocket we can lay hand to, and . . . '

The President waved a hand to silence him.

General Llewellyn sat back. His throat hurt from arguing, his hand ached from pounding the table.

At eight am, the spaceship detached a thousand-foot scout as it passed over the New Jersey coast. The scout drifted down over Washington, DC. At eight-eighteen am, the scout contacted Washington airport in perfect English, asked for landing instructions. A startled tower operator warned the scout ship off until Army units had cleared the area.

General Llewellyn and a group of expendable assistants were chosen to greet the invaders. They were at the field by eight-fifty-one. The scout, a pale robin's-egg blue, settled to a landing strip which cracked beneath it. Small apertures began flicking open and shut on the ship's surface. Long rods protruded, withdrew. After ten minutes of this, a portal opened and a ramp shot out, tipped to the ground. Again silence.

Every weapon the armed services could muster was trained on the invader. A flight of jets swept overhead. Far above them, a lone bomber circled, in its belly THE BOMB. All waited for the general's signal.

Something moved in the shadow above the ramp. Four human figures appeared at the portal. They wore striped trousers, cutaways, glistening black shoes, top hats. Their linen shone. Three carried briefcases, one had a scroll. They moved down the ramp.

General Llewellyn and aides walked out to the foot of the ramp. *They look like more bureaucrats*, thought the general.

The one with the scroll, a dark-haired man with narrow face, spoke first. 'I have the honor to be the ambassador from Krolia, Loo Mogasayvidiantu.' His English was faultless. He extended the scroll. 'My credentials.'

General Llewellyn accepted the scroll, said, 'I am General Henry A. Llewellyn' – he hesitated – 'representative of Earth.'

The Krolian bowed. 'May I present my staff?' He turned. 'Ayk Turgotokikalapa, Min Sinobayatagurki and William R. Jones, late of Boston, Earth.'

The general recognized the man whose picture was in

all of the morning newspapers. *Here's our first Solar quisling*, he thought.

'I wish to apologize for the delay in our landing,' said the Krolian ambassador. 'Occasionally quite a long period of time is permitted to elapse between preliminary and secondary phases of a colonial program.'

Colonial program! thought the general. He almost gave the signal which would unleash death upon this scene. But the ambassador had more to say.

'The delay in landing was a necessary precaution,' said the Krolian. 'Over such a long period of time our data sometimes becomes outmoded. We needed time for a sampling, to talk to Mr Jones, to bring our data up to date.' Again he bowed with courtly politeness.

Now General Llewellyn was confused: *Sampling . . . data . . .* He took a deep breath. Conscious of the weight of history on his shoulders, he said, 'We have one question to ask you, Mr Ambassador. Do you come as friends or conquerors?'

The Krolian's eyes widened. He turned to the Earthman beside him. 'It is as I expected, Mr Jones.' His lips thinned. 'That Colonial Office! Understaffed! Inefficient! Bumbling . . . '

The general frowned. 'I don't understand.'

'No, of course,' said the ambassador. 'But if our Colonial Office had kept track . . . ' He waved a hand. 'Look around at your people, sir.'

The general looked first at the men behind the ambassador. Obviously human. At a gesture from the Krolian, he turned to the soldiers behind himself, then toward the frightened faces of the civilians behind the airport fences. The general shrugged, turned back to the Krolian. 'The people of Earth are waiting for the answer to my question. Do you come as friends or conquerors?'

The ambassador sighed. 'The truth is, sir, that the question really has no answer. You must surely notice that we are of the same breed.'

The general waited.

'It should be obvious to you,' said the Krolian, 'that we have already occupied Earth . . . about seven thousand years ago.'

Panther Science Fiction – A Selection from the World's Best S.F. List

GREYBEARD	Brian W. Aldiss	40p	☐
THE MOMENT OF ECLIPSE	Brian W. Aldiss	35p	☐
LONG WAY HOME	Paul Anderson	50p	☐
THE DISASTER AREA	J. G. Ballard	30p	☐
NOW WAIT FOR LAST YEAR	Philip K. Dick	50p	☐
CLANS OF THE ALPHANE MOON	Philip K. Dick	50p	☐
THE ZAP GUN	Philip K. Dick	40p	☐
ALL THE SOUNDS OF FEAR	Harlan Ellison	30p	☐
THE TIME OF THE EYE	Harlan Ellison	35p	☐
THE RING OF RITORNEL	Charles L. Harness	35p	☐
THE CENTAURI DEVICE	M. John Harrison	50p	☐
THE MACHINE IN SHAFT TEN	M. John Harrison	50p	☐
WAR WITH THE ROBOTS	Harry Harrison	50p	☐
THE VIEW FROM THE STARS	Walter M. Miller Jr.	35p	☐
MASQUE OF A SAVAGE MANDARIN	Philip Bedford Robinson	35p	☐
THE MULLER-FOKKER EFFECT	John Sladek	35p	☐
THE STEAM-DRIVEN BOY	John Sladek	35p	☐
LET THE FIRE FALL	Kate Wilhelm	35p	☐
BUG-EYED MONSTERS	Edited by Anthony Cheetham	40p	☐

All these books are available at your local bookshop or newsagent, or can be ordered direct from the publisher. Just tick the titles you want and fill in the form below.

Name...

Address...

....

Write to Panther Cash Sales, PO Box 11, Falmouth, Cornwall TR10 9EN.

Please enclose remittance to the value of the cover price plus:

UK: 18p for the first book plus 8p per copy for each additional book ordered to a maximum charge of 66p.

BFPO and EIRE: 18p for the first book plus 8p per copy for the next 6 books, thereafter 3p per book.

OVERSEAS: 20p for the first book and 10p for each additional book.

Granada Publishing reserve the right to show new retail prices on covers, which may differ from those previously advertised in the text or elsewhere.